THE KRINAR ECLIPSE

A KRINAR WORLD NOVEL

LAUREN SMITH

For Anna,
She let me dream and write in her amazing Krinar world.

PROLOGUE

F *ive years ago*
Bianca's sweet sixteenth birthday should have been celebrated with a new car in the driveway with a pretty bow on it, *not* with an imminent alien invasion. Instead of Bianca rushing out the door, shiny new keys in hand, two Secret Service agents rushed into her bedroom and hustled her into the hallway toward her father's room.

"We have secured Hummingbird. Repeat, we have secured Hummingbird," one agent said into his ear mic. The two armed men trapped her near the back wall of her father's bedroom, shielding her with their bodies.

"Bianca?" Her father rushed over to her, his own security detail flanking him. "Are you all right?"

"I'm fine…" Her voice shook as she looked around the room. "What's going on?"

"A ship has appeared in orbit, just outside our atmosphere."

"A ship? What do you mean, *a ship*?" Bianca stared at her father's ashen face. There was really only one possible answer, but she had to hear it for herself.

"A spaceship."

Bianca would have laughed if it wasn't for the looks on the faces of the men around her. No one was joking.

"You mean…like aliens?" Her heart raced so violently in her chest that it hurt. She struggled to process what was happening.

"Yes, we—" Her father's words were cut off as a man materialized in front of them in the center of the room with a flash of light. The man—or alien, presumably—looked straight at her father.

The Secret Service agents drew their guns on the sudden intruder. Bianca just stared at the man—who looked human, yet was somehow too *perfect* to be human—as he spoke to her father. This was no thin green specter with oval-shaped black eyes who'd dropped to Earth in a beam of light from a flying saucer. This…*creature* looked more like he'd stepped off the cover of a fashion magazine. It didn't make sense. Why would aliens look so human?

His speech was slow and measured, with a hint of an accent she'd never heard before. Her stomach knotted, and her body flushed with a rush of heat as she stared, bewitched, at the beautiful man before her. She was only sixteen, but her hormones were already raging. She knew a sexy man when she saw one, and this one was *beyond* sexy.

"President Wells, I know you spoke to Arus, one of my kind, a few minutes ago, and he made it clear that we, the Krinar people, are no threat to you." The man was tall, too tall, with russet hair and brown eyes that seemed to flash a tawny gold every few seconds. There was something terrifying and fascinating about him that made it impossible to look away.

"I did speak with Arus. Who are you?" her father asked.

"My name is Soren. Arus has assigned me the role of..." Soren paused, his lips twitching in a near smile as he seemed to search for the right word. "Ambassador."

Bianca strained to see over the shoulders of her Secret Service detail. They wedged her between their two large bodies and the wall, smothering her with fear and panic as wild thoughts of a hundred alien invasion movies swarmed in her head. There was a soft rumble to the man's deep voice that seemed to put her at ease as her instincts screamed that nothing was calming about facing off with an alien.

In fact, she knew without a doubt that something was terribly wrong, because she should have been screaming and trying to escape...yet her voice wouldn't work. She was rooted to the spot in horror and fascination.

"I am to represent the needs of the Krinar people on Earth. Any issues that arise will be dealt with by me." The man crossed the room and seated himself in an armchair, the one her father liked to sit in at night and smoke a cigar when he had the chance.

"You have been poor custodians of such a precious planet. You have ruined it. We are here to fix what we can, and you will be thankful for the intervention."

This man...alien...who called himself Soren, simply leaned back, hands on the armrests in a picture of complete ease, watching them without fear. His casual, carefree attitude warned Bianca that whoever these Krinar were, they weren't afraid of humans at all. That meant they had power, and lots of it.

Soren cleared his throat politely and continued. "I assume you don't mind if I procure a residence close to yours. It will give me time to acclimate. I have not set foot on your world in more than five thousand years." Soren chuckled. "Much has changed."

Her father seemed to recover himself. "Five *thousand* years?"

"Yes. I was checking in on your progress. Egypt was the center of advanced technology. They were quite gifted."

"Our progress?" Bianca spoke up, only to have one

of her agents mutter a curse and try to remove her from the room. But she dug in her heels.

"Stop. Leave her be." Soren's commanding voice stilled the agent gripping her, and his hold loosened. "Who is this?" Soren seemed to notice her for the first time. Her father stepped between her and the Krinar man.

"My daughter, Bianca. She normally wouldn't be in here, but your little magic act has my security team noticeably concerned, and they thought it best to bring her to my room." Her father waved at the agents hovering near him and Bianca.

Soren raised a dark brow, studying Bianca. There was a knowing look in his gaze, as though he could read every thought she'd ever had. There would be no keeping secrets from him. A sudden shiver rippled down her spine at the thought of feeling so powerless against a man like him.

"Today is your birthday?" he asked as he looked down at his palm. Had he written notes on it, like she did when she was worried she'd forget something? The idea of a powerful alien needing to scribble down notes on his hand struck her as both funny and bizarre.

"Y–yes," she replied. He then moved a few steps closer, and she saw that his palm was empty of notes. What had he been looking at? And how had he known about her birthday?

"Happy birthday, then. Sixteen is an important year in a human's life, I'm told." Soren smiled and turned his focus back to her father, having lost all interest in her.

"Now, Mr. President, it's time we talked peace terms in order to prevent millions of innocent deaths." He rose with confidence and preternatural grace from the armchair and came face-to-face with her father. "Here's how Earth is going to surrender to Krinar control." Bianca felt like she'd swallowed her tongue whole as she stared at the gorgeous, scary-as-hell man who had just announced that his people were not only invading, but had already won. All she could think was that he reminded her of a leopard she'd once seen in a zoo. So close against the glass, golden eyes hungry with dark intent...

A predator.

Bianca opened her mouth to scream, but no sound came out.

1

Bianca bolted upright in bed, heart smashing against her ribs. Her roommate, Claudia, stared at her. The other girl flipped on the light between their two beds and watched her nervously.

"You'd have that dream about *him* again?" Claudia asked, her blue eyes wide. Bianca nodded. Mortification deadened her limbs as she realized she'd woken up her roommate with her screaming.

Today was her twenty-first birthday, and like clockwork, the nightmares had come back. K-Day. The day the Krinar had arrived and taken over. Everything that Bianca had believed about her life and even Earth itself had been turned on its head once the Krinar had made some announcements to the world.

Thousands of years ago, the Krinar had modified existing life on Earth to become compatible with and originate from Krinar-based DNA in order to create humans. Humans were nothing more than ants in an ant farm to them. She couldn't help but fear the day one of those Ks would give their little ant farm called Earth a mighty shake.

"I'm just glad the agents have the night off," she muttered.

Claudia nodded. The first couple of times she'd had nightmares, her agents had rushed into the room, guns drawn. Claudia had almost asked for a new roommate from Princeton's college housing. But Bianca had convinced her not to, and they'd told the agents they had to take nights off. All that really meant was that they took up a post in an SUV parked in front of the dorm. At least from there they couldn't hear her scream. She had to wear her panic button around her wrist at all times. She was glad the White House tech team had been able to make it so small. Embedded in a leather bracelet, it looked more like a fashion accessory than a personal security device.

Claudia slipped out of bed and headed into their shared bathroom. "Want me to get you some water?"

Bianca rubbed her eyes and drew in a slow breath. She wasn't sixteen anymore. She was finishing her final year at Princeton. She wasn't helpless, wasn't trapped beneath Soren's predatory gaze. Yet even after five years, thoughts of him, the first Krinar she'd ever seen, wouldn't go away. Her stomach knotted, and she suppressed a moan as she fought off the wave of nausea that came with it.

Flashes of memories, slices of that moment always came back. Predatory golden-brown eyes that threatened to swallow her whole. After she had seen him, heard his calm demands all those years ago, she had been escorted to her room and kept under lock and key while her father, the president, had spoken with him for the next four hours about the future of mankind and how best to protect the American people from panicking. It was why her father had been reelected by a landslide. He'd kept the Great Panic that had followed the invasion limited. America and the other major countries of the world had kept the confusion and casualties as low as possible.

"Here." Claudia held out a glass of water, which Bianca gratefully accepted. She curled her fingers around the glass and drank deeply. There was something purifying about water after she had nightmares, as it washed away the metallic tang in her mouth that always accompanied her nightmares.

"It's been five years. You'd think you'd have adjusted by now," said Claudia.

"You weren't there," said Bianca. "I didn't have any kind of warning to cushion the blow like most people did."

"I can't believe you were up close to *Soren*, on K-Day no less." Claudia sat cross-legged on the bed and ran her fingers through her red hair. Now she was awake and wanted to talk, but Bianca just wanted to curl up in a ball and try to make the dreams go away. Ever since K-Day, she had seen Soren *everywhere*. His arrogant, handsome face appeared on TV interviews, magazine covers, and internet articles.

The Krinar male was handsome, she could acknowledge that, but she hated him. Hated him because he'd been the first person to really look at her and then just as quickly dismiss her. She was one small, meaningless part of a race his had experimented on over eons. Just a kid. But now? She wasn't a kid anymore. What would he think of her if they came face-to-face again after all these years? She hoped she'd never know. Going to college had helped her avoid most of her father's political functions. Her mother had died before he took office, and Bianca had taken the unofficial position of her father's "plus one" to every gala and state dinner. But after the Krinar invaded, she'd been invited to fewer and fewer of those events for safety reasons, which was fine by her.

"Soren's so intimidating," Claudia continued. "But in kind of a *hot* way, you know? Like if he kissed you, you would just melt through the floor. My sister's friend went to an X-club, you know. And wow, she can't even talk about it. She gets this dazed, swoony look on her face."

That had Bianca sitting up. "Your sister knows someone who went to an X-club?"

Those were Krinar sex clubs. Well, that's what the news called them, but Bianca wasn't so certain. They were clubs run by the Ks, but they let humans come inside. The only humans who tended to go in were xenophiles, or K obsessed humans, which was why the clubs were called X-clubs. And once a human went inside, the odds of him or her ending up in a K's bed were high. Bianca knew why.

As the president's daughter, she had been educated about the Krinar more than just about anyone in the general public. She knew only too well which rumors were true and which weren't. The worst details about the Krinar, well, those were the ones that were mostly true.

The Krinar drank human blood. Not often, but they did it when having sex. Apparently it gave them some kind of pleasure high, and humans were similarly affected, like being given ecstasy that enhanced their sexual arousal beyond imagining. That wasn't something Bianca wanted to think about. The Ks were basically space vampires—not that she'd ever say that to their faces.

"Mandy said that her friend Lucy was sore for *days*." Claudia pointed discreetly below her waist.

"Seriously?"

"She didn't say *where*, though," Claudia giggled.

Bianca wished she wasn't fascinated, but she was. She was still a virgin, thanks to her agents. Any man who got too handsy with her was escorted home by her assigned Secret Service watchdogs. Daddy's orders.

"Oh yeah. She says she doesn't really remember much about what happened after one bit her, just that she was in some crazy kind of orgy."

"*Orgy?* Come on, Claudia, be serious." Bianca laughed. Orgies? Was she kidding?

"I *am* serious." Claudia frowned. "She slept with three guys, at least she thinks it was three. They were in some basement, and the furniture was floating."

Bianca snorted. Sadly, there wasn't an extra pillow on her bed to throw at her roommate. She was totally pulling her leg.

"Orgies and floating furniture? Why don't we just go back to sleep? We have two weeks until finals, and we should focus on that, not Krinar X-clubs and floating furniture."

Claudia huffed and turned off the light. Bianca settled back in her bed, pulled the covers up to her chin, and closed her eyes. But tonight she knew she would get little sleep, because Soren was there, a seductive, threatening shadow in the back of her mind. She stated known facts in her head to calm down.

Ks can't read minds. Truth.

Ks can't watch you sleep in your bed. Truth.

But they could see you in your dorm room if they decided to put cameras in here. Scary truth.

Soren doesn't know where you are, and he doesn't care. You're just the human president's brat he met once five years ago. Truth? She hoped so.

She drifted into a light, restless sleep and wondered why she couldn't shake the sense that someone was indeed watching her.

———

SOREN FROWNED AT THE HOLOGRAM OF THE HUMAN woman's dorm room, watching her toss and turn over the next three hours. He hadn't tapped into this feed in nearly four years, not since he'd assured himself that her college accommodations were suitable. She was the daughter of a great leader whom he respected, after all. It was only natural to check on her. For security. The anti-K rebels had been known to target pro-Krinar leaders and their families. The president wasn't exactly pro-Krinar, but he was supportive of peaceful relations and cooperation between their species.

Soren stared at the hologram of Bianca, and his frown deepened. Why she held such a curiosity for him, he didn't know. Perhaps because he knew she was curious about him, frightened by him too. After eight thousand long years of life, nothing much surprised or intrigued him these days. But she did. And it wasn't simply because she had grown up from a young human girl to an enchanting woman. Five years made quite a difference. He hadn't looked at her at sixteen the way he looked at her now. Now she was a grown woman.

Her long blonde hair was so unlike the dark shades of brown of his own people, and her eyes were almost a jade-like green with a hint of hazel. This was not an eye color one would see on his planet, Krina. They all had brown eyes, which sometimes warmed to gold whenever they experienced strong emotions.

Bianca Wells. He pulled up her course schedule on the Princeton servers to review the details. Her classes were all biology or zoology related. She would be obtaining her degree in a few weeks. If he understood the college servers' information correctly, she wished to become a marine biologist.

Interesting.

He leaned back in his chair, thinking. Earth had developed differently than Krina. His home world had but one giant land mass surrounded by a vast ocean. It was too dangerous to live closer than twenty miles from the shore because the strong tides were comparable to tsunamis on Earth. But here on the little blue planet with its separate continents and its many seas, they had the safety to explore it, to plumb its depths and swim alongside its creatures.

What would Bianca think if he showed her Krina

and the frightening dark pull of its dangerous waters? But he couldn't, wouldn't. He had to keep his distance. The last thing he needed was to find himself in charge of a charl, or what his people called a human companion. While the idea teased him with arousal he hadn't felt in years, he could not take the US president's daughter as his human pleasure companion. It would be seen as an act of war by President Wells, a violation of the Coexistence Treaty, and it would give the anti-Ks all the more reason to redouble their efforts to oust the Krinar from the planet, no matter that the Krinar were here to help them, to keep them from foolishly destroying their gift of a healthy planet and the young sun in their solar system. His people on Krina were on borrowed time. Their own sun in their system was dying, which had driven them to desperation, but fortunately this move to Earth had been eons in the making.

Soren turned off the screen, removing the temptation of Bianca from his mind for now.

"Soren?" Arus's voice came through the tablet on his desk. He waved a hand, activating the small implant in his palm that was connected with his mind. He could turn things on and off as well as perform other tasks in his home with thought alone.

Arus's face appeared on the screen.

"Arus, what may I help you with?" he asked the Krinar Council member.

"Two of our scientists have been accepted by several universities to start teaching Krinar history and basic science. I have a list of universities I would like them to visit. I'd like you to introduce our two teachers to the first university they will be teaching at this fall. Is this acceptable for you?"

"Of course." Soren didn't ask Arus why he wanted Soren to essentially babysit a couple of scientists, assuming Arus must have his reasons.

"Thank you. I've sent you the list of universities and the personnel files of our team members who will be meeting with you. They will arrive tomorrow morning."

"Very good," Soren replied. He was about to sever the connection when Arus spoke again. "I understand President Wells's daughter is attending one of the schools. Princeton. I believe you should request her to accompany you on the tour. It will provide good publicity if the campus sees Bianca Wells walking around with our people."

Soren cleared his throat, his blood humming with forbidden desire. "Are you sure?" He had just promised himself that he would leave Bianca alone, and now Arus was serving the delicious little woman to him on a platter. It would be impossible not to have a small taste of the pleasure she would give any male who took her to bed. He'd gone too long without a companion, had even gone too long without sharing his bed. He and his people had no sexual taboos the way humans did. They viewed sex as a thing to be shared and enjoyed, which made his relative celibacy rare. One did not need to have a partner or be in a lasting relationship to indulge. In the last five years, Soren's hungers and desires had been dormant. Seeing her tonight had brought his hard-edged arousal back to the surface.

"I'm certain. Bring Wells's daughter," Arus confirmed. Then his face vanished as he severed the connection.

Soren closed his eyes, drawing in a deep breath. It would take everything in him not to take Bianca tomorrow, *take* her and taste her. He entertained the thought of contacting an old female friend, someone to come and satisfy his urges, but that would not take the edge off the hunger that had stirred to life after seeing Bianca in bed tonight. He remembered how she had turned and kicked off her covers, revealing sleek, curvy legs and a bottom he wanted to sink his teeth into. And then there was the delicious curve of her neck and the slopes of her breasts beneath the loose cotton T-shirt she wore. What he wouldn't give to strip her bare and fuck the life out of her until her throat was raw from screaming in pleasure.

In eight thousand years, he'd never known a temptation like Bianca Wells.

2

____

"That's weird…" Bianca stared at the inbox of her school email on her phone before putting on her short black ankle boots and pulling her jeans down over them.

Claudia lounged on her bed, a fat biochemistry book open in front of her and a fleet of slender Post-it notes scattered like brightly colored flower petals around her. "What's weird?"

"The university president just emailed me. He has some special guests coming on campus today. He wants me to join them on a tour."

"You *are* the president's daughter. I'm surprised Ackerman even kept his promise not to trot you out like a prized pony this long." Claudia highlighted something in her book, still not looking up.

"I know. Mr. Ackerman has been pretty low-key up

till now." She remembered her interview day, when the only question she'd had for him had been whether she would be able to feel like a normal college kid and not have her life on display to entertain big donors and that sort of thing. He had promised her that he would let her have a quiet, completely normal experience.

"Maybe since I'm only a few weeks away from graduating, he felt he could break his promise."

Claudia made a noise as though she was listening, but Bianca knew better. Claudia was deep into prepping for her biochemistry finals and couldn't afford any distractions. Bianca left her roommate alone and met her Secret Service agents, Mike and Scott, as she left her dorm room.

They'd been with her for the last four years, and were more like overprotective brothers than armed agents. They wore dark sunglasses and had the telltale little radios plugged in their ears.

Mike put his hand to his mouth, whispering as he communicated with another team off campus. "Hummingbird on the move." And then they were off, like a three-part machine, moving in tandem across campus. The agents didn't wear suits—they wore street clothes to keep attention to a minimum—but it was hard not to notice the two grim-faced men trailing close behind her.

When she was sixteen, she had hated the agents following her everywhere, but now she had grown used to them. They really weren't that bad, and they didn't completely destroy her social life. In recent years they'd eased up on her detail, probably because the threat to her life had decreased after K-Day. When the Krinar invaded, politics had changed on the global scale. The Ks were the *real* threat, and the rebellious factions of humans across the globe had become more united against them.

"Slight change in plans, guys," she told the agents as she steered away from the student union and headed toward the administrative building.

Scott frowned. "Oh?" He didn't like change because it could put her in danger if he couldn't clear a room or a setting before she arrived there safely.

"Mr. Ackerman wants me to join him on some tour around campus. He must have some heavy donors he wants to impress."

"He should've cleared that with the security detail last night" Mike began. Bianca put a hand on his arm and sighed.

"It's not a big deal, okay?" She trotted up the steps to the administration building and went inside.

Mr. Ackerman's office was on the first floor in a corner suite. Bianca smiled at his receptionist while she called the president on the phone. She listened to whatever he said and then nodded eagerly.

"Just have a seat, Ms. Wells. They'll be right out."

Bianca sat down, and the two agents hovered

nearby, one at the door and the other in the hallway. She summoned a polite smile as the door opened and President Ackerman stepped out of his office, but her smile faltered as she noticed who was behind him. Two Krinar, one a svelte female and the other an attractive, muscled male. Then her heart stopped as she caught sight of another Krinar male leaving the office.

Ambassador Soren is here. She felt dizzy with a sudden spell of vertigo.

"Ms. Wells, such a delight to have you accompanying us today…" Ackerman continued speaking, but she could barely understand him. Her head was buzzing as she drank in the sight of the man who'd starred in far too many of her dreams *and* nightmares. He wore a fitted light-gray pair of trousers and a black sweater that molded to his body enough to indicate his muscled physique. Other than his clothes, he hadn't changed one bit since she'd last seen him. The Krinar didn't age, she knew that, but she didn't know how that was possible. But he was an alien, and there was much humans didn't know about the Krinar. They kept their science and technology incredibly secret.

Soren was the creature of her nightmares, but he was also the only man she'd ever had sexual fantasies about, intense ones—sometimes dark ones that made her wake shivering and hungry for things that filled her with shame. Yet she couldn't deny the raw passion that thoughts of him could incite in her. It made it hard to take other men seriously when they asked her out because the only man she could think about was him.

It was messed up, but it was the truth. And it was something she wanted to bury out of sight. But that wouldn't be possible today. Not with the simmering heat coming from Soren as he looked into her eyes.

"Ms. Wells?" Ackerman's voice broke through the chaos of her thoughts.

She blushed. "Sorry, President Ackerman."

"This is Jaks." He nodded toward the male K, who smiled pleasantly at her. "And this is Driana." The female's smile was also warm and genuine. "You are familiar with Ambassador Soren, I believe?"

All she could manage was a nod.

"Good. Well, Jaks and Driana are going to start lectures this fall at Princeton. Ambassador Soren knew you attended here and believed it might be beneficial to share your experiences with our new professors."

Knowing this was not a time she could turn and escape, she had to grin and bear the situation as best she could. She stepped up to Driana, and Driana trailed the backs of her knuckles down Bianca's left cheek in greeting. Bianca returned it. "It's nice to meet you." She had learned the Krinar greeting years ago. She stepped toward Jaks to do the same, but he gave a slight shake of his head when Soren made a low sound that sounded suspiciously like a growl. Was he honest to God growling? Jaks didn't look Soren's way, but his smile was still warm as he nodded in greeting instead.

Soren didn't approach her, and for that she was thankful. If he had touched her, she honestly didn't know what she would have done. He continued to watch her, his eyes giving her body an invisible caress that made her break out in goosebumps.

Ackerman cleared his throat. "Well...er...shall we start the tour?"

For the next two hours, she and Ackerman worked together to present the prestigious history of Princeton and answer any questions the Ks had about the university and college life. Jaks and Driana were polite and clearly interested in the human college experience. Soren remained silent except when the other Ks asked him something. The entire time, his focus remained fixed on her. Her blood heated beneath her skin each time she glanced his way and found him intensely watching her. This was so different from five years ago. She'd been dismissed so quickly then, but now she had caught his attention and couldn't shake it.

"You enjoy living in these dormitories?" Jaks inquired as they paused before one of the many housing structures on campus. "They seem...small."

"College students enjoy being around people our own age. Sometimes it can be like a party. I like the quiet more, but my roommate, Claudia, is fun."

Driana lifted her head back as she studied the tall

red brick dorm. "In our settlements, we prefer a little more space. We spread out rather than live on top of one another." Her observation was not made with condescension but rather with curiosity.

Soren spoke up. "We are *highly* territorial, aren't we, Jaks?"

Bianca's gaze darted between the two handsome men, and she thought she saw amusement in Jaks's eyes before he replied.

"Certainly some more than others."

President Ackerman watched the exchange, clearly puzzled, before he clapped his hands together. "Right, well, the library is next."

They headed to Princeton's Firestone Library, and the Ks murmured among themselves in appreciation at the modern blend of stone and glass. Giant circular chandeliers that Claudia called "the glowing doughnuts" illuminated one of the main study areas.

"Why don't I show you our oldest archives? We have some impressive first editions of some of the greatest human literature." Ackerman led the way. Bianca knew they would come back eventually to leave, so she remained by the entryway closest to the stacks. She hoped it would give her a moment to avoid Soren while he joined them in the archives portion of the library. Only he didn't move around her, didn't go with the other Ks. He stayed right there behind her, the heat of his body so close she could feel it. Mike and

Scott shifted restlessly from their positions fifteen feet away, but she didn't call for help.

"It has been a long time, Bianca," Soren said, his voice low and soft, dangerously sweet. Bianca knew better than to trust that voice, no matter how much she had fantasized about it over the years, albeit in a very different context.

"It has." She moved deeper into the stacks, not wanting any students to see them talking. Her security detail kept a discreet distance.

"And you have been well?" he asked, still in that soft, dangerous tone that made her shiver, and her thighs tightened. "When I meet with your father, he rarely speaks of you. He focuses only on business."

"Yes, he's good that way," she replied. "I don't like him to talk about me." *Especially to you,* she thought.

Soren leaned against the stacks to her left, blocking her exit. She looked up at him. She was not short by any means at five feet six inches, but Soren was six foot seven and made her feel tiny. A shiver rippled through her, and it didn't escape his notice.

"Are you cold?" He removed a device from his pocket, no bigger than a computer mouse, and before she could stop him, he pressed a button. A beam of light shot into the air, and she was shocked to see a thin pale-gray jacket materialize in front of her. He slipped the device back into his pocket and retrieved the jacket, which still hung suspended in the air, then slipped her arms into it. She knew from her father's meetings that what he used was called a fabricator. The Ks had such advanced technology that they could produce almost anything they desired using such a tiny device.

His hands lingered a moment longer on her shoulders than was appropriate for two strangers. But they weren't strangers, were they? And how often had she dreamed about him? Fantasized about those hands on her body, stroking, caressing, teasing her? Too many times. Her screams of fear all too often had turned to screams of pleasure as she'd awakened in the dark, her body dewed with sweat and her panties wet with her desire.

It always filled her with shame, to be turned on by an alien, especially the one who'd put her father in his place like a trained dog and had taken over the running of Earth so smoothly. But there was no denying the power Soren had over her in the realm of dreams. How he would trap her beneath him on a bed, pumping into her over and over, his teeth sinking into her neck, and how she'd obliterate into a thousand pieces as a primal, overwhelming climax rocked her to her core.

The way he was looking at her now, as though he could read her thoughts, made his eyes flash gold and his lips part slightly. His warm breath fanned her face, and she trembled at the heat building between them. It was as though they were at the heart of a dying star, spirals of light spinning outward from them. She'd seen that once on a science show, and she'd never forgotten the beautiful image. Now she felt as if she were living that within that moment.

He slowly released her but didn't move away.

"You...you didn't need to do that." She wished she could shrug off the clothing made by his alien technology. But the jacket fit perfectly. Of course it did. Everything the Ks did was perfect, right down to controlling the lives of humans. She was all too aware of the fact that right now he could do anything to her that he liked, and it wouldn't be against any of the laws because Ks were above human laws. *They* were in charge.

"There's far more pleasure in doing what one *wants* than what one *needs*, don't you agree?" He brushed his knuckles down her cheek in greeting, but unlike with Driana, it was not an innocent gesture. His touch left a burning sensation on her skin that made her head spin, and he leaned down until their faces were a few inches apart. His brown eyes swirled into honey gold again, and his dark, masculine scent surrounded her. He repeated the light caress to her other cheek, and she couldn't stop herself from reacting. When she leaned into that touch, he stopped breathing for a few seconds, and so did she.

Her eyes locked with his, and her desire for him,

the thing she hated most about herself, seemed too strong to fight.

"You tempt me, Bianca. Tempt me to break my own rules."

She stared at his full lips now, fascinated by the sensual curve of them as he smiled. "What rules?"

"I didn't want to get involved with a human, especially not one as politically important as you, but..." He cupped her chin, his face moving even closer. "But it seems I can't deny myself."

It was the only warning she had before his lips stole hers. The kiss exploded with the force of a bursting supernova. His lips nibbled at hers, his tongue winning entrance to her mouth. He tasted so good, unexpectedly sweet, which Bianca puzzled over as she gripped his sweater to draw him closer. The thrill of his kiss startled her so much that she didn't resist, didn't push away. No, her treacherous body burrowed closer to his, and his low, purring approval flushed her body from head to toe with spirals of wild heat. Her pulse pounded as he moved his head lower to her throat. He flicked his tongue against her skin before dragging the tips of his sharp teeth along her neck, causing a light rasping sensation.

A moan so loud it mortified her escaped her lips as she grew wet. His teeth moved to the crook between her neck and shoulder, sinking slightly deeper. Was he going to bite her?

"Please..." Bianca breathed a plea, but she honestly wasn't sure if she was asking him to stop or to keep going.

"Please what, *lilana*?" He gathered her into his arms, and the scent of him washing over her made her delightfully dizzy.

"What does that mean? *Lilana?*"

Soren nuzzled her neck, his lips moving in soft whispers over her skin. "It means *precious one* in my tongue."

Precious one? How could she be precious to him? He was a K, and she was human. She knew how he viewed her people. His words from five years ago to her father still echoed in her head.

"You have been poor custodians of such a precious planet. You have ruined it. We are here to fix what we can, and you will be thankful for the intervention."

The memory was a cold slap to her face. She flattened her palms on his chest and shoved. Hard. The muscled mass of Soren's tall form didn't budge. Tears of rage and shame pricked her eyes. She hated being weak, and only Soren made her feel like this. She was helpless around him, a toy, nothing of consequence.

He pulled back and stared down at her, concern darkening his eyes. His russet hair, a rare color among the Krinar, fell into his eyes. Had he been any other man, she would have reached up to brush it away from his beautiful, predatory eyes. But she didn't dare. His pull was undeniable, and to touch him would be to risk everything.

"Ms. Wells, are you all right?" Scott asked.

The agent's voice drew her eyes away from Soren. Scott and Mike hovered like overprotective mother hens. A fresh wave of mortification rolled through her. She had been caught making out in the stacks like some college freshman, with a damned Krinar! And her agents, two men she trusted with her life, were frowning in disapproval, their faces pale, and each looked ready to draw his weapon.

"I...I'm fine." She gave the agents a grateful smile, but they all knew that if they dared to attack or restrain Soren, he was capable of ripping them to pieces. Krinar were incredibly fast and strong.

Everyone had seen the footage of a Middle Eastern terrorist cell that had tried to fight off just one Krinar male. The male had been hit by a sniper's bullet during a surprise attack, and that had only pissed him off. He'd rushed their position and torn them to pieces with his bare hands in a blood-fueled rage. If Soren wanted her, Mike and Scott would die trying to protect her from him, but they *would* die. She wouldn't let that happen. She would surrender to him if she had to in order to protect those two good men.

"Will the tour be over soon?" Soren asked, ignoring the agents.

"I think so. Ackerman doesn't have much else to show them."

Soren's lips curved in the ghost of a smile. "Good. When it is over, you and I shall talk." He stepped away and exited the stacks to wait in the entryway for his fellow Ks to return.

Bianca ran her hands through her hair and struggled to grip the frayed ends of her self-control. Soren wanted her. She had felt the press of his shaft against her belly as he'd kissed her, and the blazing heat in his promise of what he wished to do with her. What was she going to do? There was no escaping this.

"Bianca," Mike whispered softly, but even he knew that Soren could probably still hear them. "You sure you're okay? We can take you away, call your father"

"No!" she hissed. If they called him, he would be furious, and that would risk the peaceful relationship between Earth and Krina. The Coexistence Treaty was in place, but that didn't mean it couldn't be broken if she was foolish enough to resist. Lives could be lost, and they could be enslaved more than they were now. At least right now the human race could tolerate their situation. The Ks ran the show, but they let human lives go on mostly unaffected. But all of that could change if she dared to resist whatever Soren wanted from her.

"You sure?" Scott pressed. "He wasn't following protocol. It should be reported."

"No. You know as well as I do what that could lead to. If he comes back to my dorm, stay outside. *Please.*" She reached out to touch both men on the shoulders, but the heavy sound of a distant growl made her hands freeze inches from their skin. She drew a slow breath.

Krinar males are possessive. Truth.

Krinar males will not let another man touch what they believe is theirs. Truth.

But she wasn't his. She was her own person, and she would never belong to anyone the way Soren seemed to want her to belong to him.

She rejoined Soren in the foyer of the library just as Ackerman and the two Krinar professors returned.

"There is something so amazing about your books," Driana said with a soft, appreciative smile. "I feel sorrow for the trees destroyed, yet the books themselves with their stories and knowledge pay tribute to the plants that bore them."

Jaks nodded sagely. "Well said."

Bianca watched the two alien professors, still surprised by their genuine warmth and friendliness. She had only ever met Krinar like Soren before, the kind who dealt with politics and those who had conquered the world. It was easy to imagine the Krinar as only bloodthirsty warriors, not like these inquisitive and kind Krinar. They had shown only respect and curiosity for her world and the lives of the college students. There had been no condescension, no looking down their noses at their primitive human ways.

"Well." Ackerman smiled at the group. "I think we've seen enough today. You're welcome back anytime before August, of course. I'll have your offices prepared in the buildings belonging to your respective fields of study, medicine, and Krinar and human biology."

"Biology?" Bianca couldn't resist piping up. "Which one of you is teaching that?"

Driana grinned. "I am. Is that an interest of yours?"

"Yes!" Bianca said, forgetting for a moment about Soren, who had come up close behind her.

"I'm studying marine biology. I would love to speak with you about Krinar marine life, if you are familiar with it. I won't be here this fall since I'm graduating, so I'll miss your class. Can I meet with you instead?"

Driana's gaze drifted above Bianca's head to something behind her, the female K's expression searching for a moment before she smiled again and nodded.

"Soon. Very soon, little one," Driana promised. She held out her hand and caressed Bianca's face, and Bianca, thrilled at the prospect of talking to a Krinar biologist, returned the greeting with a smile. Her heart was bursting with excitement as she watched the university president escort Jaks and Driana away.

Then only she and Soren were left, along with her security detail.

"Show me to your dorm, Bianca." Soren's

command was gentle, but it was still an order. He reached out to catch one of her hands as he said this, his warm palm covering hers completely. She knew he wouldn't let her go if she tried to pull away. Domination shone in his gaze, even if it was gentled by a soft half smile. She bristled at his command, but she didn't say anything. She headed off to her room, her hand still entwined with his.

She was doomed. There was no preventing whatever was to come.

3
____

Soren kept his amusement at Bianca's blatant coolness in check. Perhaps that was what had drawn his attention when he'd first met her five years ago. She had challenged him, shouting questions at an alien just moments after discovering they existed. She was full of natural charm and bravado. She reminded him of his twin brother, Sef. Twins were rare in their world, but despite their identical appearance, he and Sef couldn't have been more different. But Bianca's feisty attitude was very much like Sef's.

His brother would be only too delighted to hear that Soren was growing attached to someone who didn't immediately acquiesce to his demands. At that moment, Bianca marched ahead of him like a warrior facing a battle she knew she couldn't win. Stubborn creature—she had nothing to fear from him, except perhaps having to face night after night of intense pleasure.

It was true that he'd gotten carried away in the library stacks, but he wouldn't let it happen again, not until he was certain she desired him as much as he did her. He never forced females into his bed, and Bianca would be no different. If anything, he would take more care to woo her properly. But that did mean he'd have to show her that her responses to him were natural, a good thing, not something shameful.

He ignored the looks of the students as they passed, knowing that he and a human—their president's daughter, no less—must make for quite the spectacle. It was good that she had two agents to protect her, but they were only human. He would assign a Krinar guardian to watch over her. Krinar guardians were their form of law enforcement, and they would be discreet so that no one would know they were being watched. Sef was a guardian, but he currently worked missions involving human resistance fighters, so Soren would have to find someone else.

Bianca stopped at the entrance to a red brick dormitory and nodded to her two agents. The men nodded back, then reluctantly walked away toward their parked SUV on the street.

"You've trained them well." Soren chuckled at the almost violent look that Bianca shot him.

"They're not pets. They would give their lives for

me. They're good men." She darted into the building, and he followed her inside. Her room was on the second floor, next to the main staircase. Soren waited to see the inside of the room he'd glimpsed on the camera feed last night. For some reason, everything about her life now fascinated him.

She opened the door, and a sweet smell wafted around him, a mix of Bianca's feminine aroma blended with scented hair products from her bathroom. Her hair smelled of vanilla. He had grown fond of the Earth plant and its enticing aroma. Nothing smelled like that back on his home world.

He followed her inside and shut the door behind them. Bianca shrugged out of the coat he had made for her and tried to hand it back to him.

"Here. I don't"

"I have no need for it, and it will fit only you. Keep it." He pushed the coat back against her, their hands meeting in a brief brush of skin and fabric. Her gaze fell upon their joined hands, and he admired her elegant, slender fingers. He was lost in memories of how it felt to have those fingers grasp his sweater to drag him closer. But now she pulled away from him.

"Uh... So yeah...this is my dorm. That's pretty much the last part of the tour." She waved an arm around the room before she hung up the jacket and put it in her small closet.

"Small accommodations. Don't you miss the finer,

larger rooms you enjoyed living at the White House?" He could never have survived the cramped confines of this room. Even thinking about it made his stomach twist in old fears.

He'd once traveled outside the Krinar solar system when he'd been a younger male, wanting to seek glory and respect by bringing back news of other worlds to his people. He had stopped on one planet, Zaruth, and had been captured by a primitive race. They had been armed with weapons laced with a drug he hadn't been familiar with, and before he could adapt, he'd been taken captive. For three hundred years, he'd been a captive of a primitive race. He'd escaped by the grace of good luck and cunning, but that failure was still planted firmly in his mind thousands of years later. The fear it had instilled in him was sometimes inescapable.

He shrugged off the suffocation that was building around him and forced his mind back to the present.

"I thought it would drive me crazy at first, but it's fun sharing a room with Claudia."

"Claudia..." He pretended not to recognize the name. "And she is what, exactly?"

"My roommate." Bianca crossed her arms over her chest and bit her lip. He knew she was on edge being so close to him, and rightly so. Each time she took her bottom lip between her teeth and nibbled it, it made his body throb with an ancient fire and hunger to grab her and push her down onto the bed. He could show her just how much she would enjoy belonging to him, having her body mastered and dominated while he pleasured her over and over.

I am eight thousand years old. I do not lose control over females. Certainly not ones so delicate. He repeated the reminder again in his head, not that it helped much.

"You said you are to graduate in a few weeks?" He stepped closer, and she drifted back a step, her back colliding with the wall as he worked her into a corner. He watched her breasts rise and fall rapidly, like a caged animal. It shouldn't have excited him, but the predatory part of him urged him to pounce, to take what was his. Soren clenched his fists at his sides to keep from reaching for her.

"Yes. Two weeks." Her breathless reply pleased him. He wanted to keep her off balance. He wanted her aware of the sexual tension that buzzed between them like electricity.

Soren reached up and placed a hand on the wall beside her head, leaning in as he spoke.

"Do you have a lover?" He knew the answer but wanted to see what she would say. Lie to protect herself, or dare to tell the truth?

"What? You go from asking about school to boyfriends?" She tried to slide away from him along the wall, but he used his other hand to catch her hip.

His hold was gentle, but he kept her firmly in place in front of him.

"Yes. Do you have a lover?" He repeated the question, watching the way her pupils dilated.

"Yes." She narrowed her eyes at him. "I do."

"Liar," he teased with a chuckle. She glared up at him. He rubbed his hand on her hip, slowly gentling her with his caress, but it only made the rebellious fire burn brighter in her eyes.

"Don't call me a liar!" she hissed.

"Then don't lie." His focus dropped to her lips. "Or else I'll give your mouth something else to do." *Like use it on my body,* he thought with delight. She would be the sort of female a man could kiss and tease for hours, being satisfied to explore her in all ways before finally claiming her.

She punched his chest, though it had no effect, and he leaned in even closer. He could smell her arousal and had become almost drugged with the scent.

"You arrogant ass—" Bianca was cut off as her roommate, Claudia, barged in the door, chattering wildly.

"Oh my God, did you hear, Bianca? There are Krinar on campus. They" Claudia held a tower of books almost up to her chin, and she suddenly noticed Soren. She made a startled squawk, and the heavy stack in her arms went flying. Soren reacted without hesitation, moving to catch the tumbling textbooks in a reasonably composed stack. Then he held them out to Bianca's trembling roommate.

"Um, Bee, there's a Krinar in our room. I'm not *hallucinating*, am I?" she said in a panicked whisper.

Soren almost chuckled. Aside from his immense height to give him away, his people had eyes that didn't quite look human, and their features were perhaps a little too...perfect, according to some. Humans could recognize them as aliens on some instinctive level.

"Claudia, this is Ambassador Soren. Soren, this is Claudia Putnam." When it was clear that Claudia wasn't going to take the books back, he set them on her bed and bowed.

"It's a pleasure, Ms. Putnam. I apologize for intruding upon your living quarters. I was curious about them, and Bianca graciously offered to show them to me." He could feel Bianca's mutinous glare. She hadn't offered, and they both knew it.

"It's nice to...meet you?" Claudia ended the greeting in a question, her eyes flicking between him and Bianca in concern. She didn't trust him, because Bianca had told her all too often about the nightmares she had about the invasion—or K-Day, as the humans called it. He was a part of what had left Bianca anxious and restless on so many nights. If all went well, that would change. She would still be restless at night, but for other, more pleasurable reasons. Once he showed her how good things between them could be, she would be anxious to stay in his bed and in his arms.

"Hey, Bee, are you good? You want me to leave?" Claudia was staring openly at him now, eyes wide with mixed terror and fascination.

"Stay," Bianca pleaded with her roommate. It was a cry for help, that quiet one-word utterance. Soren didn't want her afraid, but it would take time to ease her fears. She was young. Twenty-one was fully grown for humans, but he knew she had no real experience around males of her own species, let alone Krinar males. He would gently introduce her to a world of passion, show her that desire and hunger were not things to be feared.

"Okay, since this is my room too, and Bee is my friend, you're going to have to answer some questions if you want to stay," Claudia announced bravely.

Bianca's breath came out in a relieved sigh, and Soren's ears picked up on the faint *flush–thump–flush–thump* of her heartbeat as that sweet blood of hers rushed through her veins.

Soren moved his focus from Bianca's blood to her roommate.

"Ask. I can't guarantee to answer all your questions —some information is classified by the non-interference mandate."

"Okay." Claudia edged slowly around him to sit on her bed. Bianca did the same, curling up on her own bed. This allowed Soren to claim Bianca's desk chair as he prepared for the roommate's inquisition.

"First off, what's this non-interference mandate?" Claudia asked. "Is that like the Prime Directive from *Star Trek*?"

Soren glanced at Bianca, knowing that she knew the answer, but he indulged her roommate's curiosity.

"It's a set of rules we have imposed on ourselves about limiting our interference in human evolution. Revealing certain bits of knowledge, technology, or even healing humans who aren't our chosen companions can be considered a violation. There are some of my people, the KETHS, or the Krinar for Ethical Treatment of Humans, who are pushing to have the mandate updated now that we've contacted and are coexisting with you. They seek to have your medical knowledge advanced in order to cure more illnesses based on what we know of human biology."

"Why would you worry about interfering in our evolution?" Bianca asked. Soren wanted to praise her for losing her animosity, at least for now.

He leaned back, getting comfortable in his chair. "Given that we set your existence in motion, we have been monitoring you over the eons, but we have tried our best to let you grow and adapt on your own to your own world. It's only now, when we've seen signs of economic and resource mismanagement, that we chose to intervene so you could stop destroying your world."

He expected the girls to have a dozen follow-up questions on that, but Bianca and Claudia exchanged glances before Claudia asked a somewhat unexpected question.

"What is a charl? Is it true that they are human sex slaves for Ks?"

Soren resisted the urge to roll his eyes, a human habit he'd picked up. "We have no sex slaves. That is foolish anti-K propaganda."

"But you do have charls. We all saw the broadcast of that girl from New York. She married one of you."

"Mia and her cheren named Korum were married, yes," he confirmed, well aware of the unusual situation. It was the first time a Krinar had married a human, following human customs, no less, to show a lifelong bond. Something stirred deep in Soren. In all his years, he'd never once sought to bind himself to any female the way his friend Korum had done with Mia. Korum had proven his devotion to his charl by going through with a human ceremony.

Soren's gaze drifted back to Bianca, tracing her full lips, delicate nose, golden brows that arched above those rare, green human eyes. She had no idea how beautiful she was or how she made his blood hum and his heart pound at the thought of gathering her in his arms. A deep longing, one he had buried for centuries, made his chest ache. He resisted the urge to rub his chest over his heart.

"*Charl* is hard to translate into human terms, but what comes closest is 'one who pleases.'"

"Charls are always human?" Bianca asked quietly.

"Yes. The word is special, reserved only for lifelong human companions of my people. Humans are charls, and the Krinar they belong to are called cheren." He met Bianca's green gaze as she narrowed her eyes.

"Do *you* have a charl?"

He waited a heartbeat too long to answer on purpose, long enough to see the flare in her eyes and a flash of jealousy, which made him smile.

"No, *lilana*, I have no charl. I've never had a charl."

"Interesting..." Claudia drummed her fingertips on her chin, her dark-red hair tumbling around her. She reminded him a little of those Pomeranian dogs he'd seen walking about the neighborhood of his residence in Washington. *Humans and their pets...* He hadn't understood the need to keep an animal, but over time he had come to realize that most domesticated dogs were not simply there to entertain humans. They worked as part of the pack, fitting in with humans in their lives, helping them in many ways. Soren, having lived so long, was now better able to process why humans did the puzzling things they did.

"So, this was fun, but I have class," Claudia said a little too casually as she got off her bed and retrieved her bag from the floor. "But I'll see you tonight, Bianca. To, you know…" She headed for the door but paused at the doorway. "You sure you're okay?"

"I'm fine—don't worry about me," Bianca said. "We're just about done here."

Claudia nodded. "If you're sure. My Mace is in the nightstand drawer." And with that, she left them alone.

Bianca remained silent for a long moment before her eyes slowly slid to the drawer in question.

"Mace would not affect me," he warned. "But it is good that your roommate cares for your well-being."

Her shoulders sagged in resigned defeat. This was not how he wished her to be.

"I would never hurt you." Why he felt the need to tell her this he wasn't sure, but she seemed convinced he was an evil alien bent on seducing her against her will. He wouldn't. But he would prove to her that her desire for him was very real. What existed between them, the flame, that was rare, once-in-a-lifetime rare. If she wanted to walk away from him, she had to know what she would be abandoning first.

"What are you doing this evening with your friend?" he inquired.

She met his stare, defiantly lifting her chin in challenge. "Oh, just dinner out. Girl time."

Did she think he would make some command that she stay home? Well, he was a bit strict, perhaps, but not unreasonable. She would know soon enough what it meant to belong to him, but not yet. The hunt would be sweeter the longer he delayed the gratification of claiming her. But he would. He'd decided that in the library as he'd kissed her. It would be dangerous for her, and it would be an outrage for her father and possibly bring about a conflict between their races, but she was worth it. She made him feel things he'd thought long gone from his ancient existence. He wished he could say it was simply passion he felt, but there was *more*. So much more.

As he'd watched her show off her campus today, he had seen her intelligence, her pride, her knowledge. She was more than a simple source of pleasure—not that he wouldn't enjoy that part of her—she was also a worthy companion to him. She would keep him on his toes with her youthful vibrance, and he would steady and guide her with his many thousands of years of experience.

Soren stood and looked once more about the room. "Take care tonight, *lilana*."

He left without allowing himself to steal a kiss or a tempting touch. He had a busy night ahead with important matters in DC. But he had accomplished one thing. As he'd kissed her in the library, he'd grasped her wrist that held the bracelet that alerted her agents of danger. He'd left his own microdot technology on the leather so he could track her. It would have been easy enough to hack the human device, but he wanted his own tech on Bianca, to know it would be precise and would not fail him. Once he had a chance to use other technology on her or plant nanocytes in her, he would be able to track her exact location. The nanocytes, while repairing her body and keeping her from aging, would also offer an advanced form of what humans call GPS. The microdot was pressed against her wrist and would measure her blood pressure and heart rate. If something happened and she was in danger, he would know instantly and hopefully be able to reach her in time to protect her.

He exited the dorm, shoving his hands in the pockets of his trousers as he walked toward the SUV where the two agents sat. He stopped in front of the car, and one agent rolled his window down.

"She's planning to go out tonight. Protect her well, or you will pay with your lives." He growled the warning in a low voice, and he knew that his eyes must have changed to gold as he tried to control his temper. The two men flinched and nodded.

Then Soren walked away into the growing dusk to where his private spacecraft was carefully hidden from human eyes.

SOMEONE WATCHED FROM THE SHADOWS. SOREN WALKED

away from the dormitory that President Wells's daughter was staying in.

So the alien parasite had taken an interest in the girl. His employer wouldn't be pleased to hear that. The president's daughter and a K? It could make the K and human alliance stronger, which was the last thing he and his employer wanted. But he had an idea about how to use the situation to their advantage. The man pulled out a cell phone and dialed a number.

"It's me," he said, eyes still fixed on the darkness where the K had vanished into the gloom like a wraith.

"Soren has left Wells's daughter's room. Do you want her removed?" He listened to the soft voice on the line.

"You know what to do. Make sure it looks like murder. Leave evidence implicating the Ks," the woman said.

"Understood." He ended the connection, deleted the call history, and then reset the phone to factory settings, making it impossible to find the number he'd dialed.

The man slunk into the shadows to prepare for tonight.

4

Bianca frowned at herself in the mirror, wishing she had Claudia's slimmer body. Her hips were just a little too large, as were her breasts.

"Damn, you look great, Bee," Claudia said from behind her. They both wore cute dresses, hers black and knee-length, Claudia's red and mid-thigh. Nothing too wild for either of them. They were just going to a bar to celebrate her twenty-first birthday since she had been busy all day with homework, the campus tour, and Soren. She definitely needed a drink to forget about that brooding Krinar and his intoxicating kisses.

"You ready? Let's get Rocky and Bullwinkle to give us a ride." Claudia had nicknamed the Secret Service agents using names from an old cartoon.

Bianca wrinkled her nose. "They really shouldn't do that. They aren't my personal drivers."

"If they drive us, it saves gas and therefore saves the ozone or whatever. The Ks will love that."

Claudia had a point, so when they left their room, they went down to the parked SUV. Scott rolled down his window.

"Scott, any chance we can get a ride to the Red Lion pub?"

"Sure, Ms. Wells." He unlocked the car doors, and she and Claudia climbed into the back. Neither agent said anything, and the girls kept quiet as well. Scott remained with them while they waited for Mike to park, and then they all entered the bar.

"So...?" Claudia prompted.

"What?"

"How did things go with Soren after I left?" Claudia applied another layer of lipstick as she waited for a response.

"Okay. He only stayed a few minutes longer." She wanted to tell her friend what had happened in the library, the way she'd felt like she was losing her mind for kissing Soren back and how she'd been afraid—not of him, but of herself.

That kiss had been dangerous. It had promised her things she hadn't even known she wanted. Heat, light, stars dotting her vision as their lips melded together. She hadn't wanted it to end, hadn't cared where she was or even who she was. Kissing Soren was like surrendering everything she was to him. She could taste the dangerous truth on his lips. He would kiss her, and it would consume her until nothing was left.

"You okay, Bee?" Claudia asked.

"I'm fine." Bianca didn't dare confess to her friend how ashamed she felt being attracted to Soren. He was the last man on Earth she should have been attracted to, but there was no escaping the fact that she was. She'd been obsessed with him since she was sixteen. Five years hadn't changed that, and neither would another five. She'd been all too aware of him, seeing him everywhere—the news, the covers of magazines, newspapers, all over social media. There were whole fan groups of girls online devoted to him, and they even called themselves Sorenites. But that was to be expected given that Soren looked like he'd just walked off the cover of *GQ* magazine or out of a Hugo Boss ad.

Bianca inwardly winced. *And I had to go and kiss him in the damn library.*

Mike and Scott chose seats at the end of the bar, ordering sodas, while she and Claudia grabbed a table near the stage. A man was playing a guitar, and a woman crooned softly into the microphone.

The music made her think of Soren. Of the way he'd held her close in his arms, his body vibrating as he'd struggled for control. She had felt that, his battle over his self-control, and she'd seen the churning gold pools of his eyes, eyes far too beautiful to be human.

The waitress paused in front of their table. "What can I get you?"

"A bourbon, neat," Claudia answered.

"And you?" the girl asked Bianca.

Bianca hadn't bothered to look at the drink menu. "Er, the same?" Her friend smirked as they offered their IDs to the waitress before she left.

She arched a brow at Claudia. "What?"

"You won't like it. Bourbon is an acquired taste."

"And you've acquired it? You're only three weeks older than me."

"Yeah, but I'm not a Goody Two-shoes like you. I've been drinking since eighteen. Not much, but enough to know what I like." Claudia peered around the bar. "What if we pick up some guys tonight?"

Bianca knew her friend was kidding. Mostly. They'd both agreed never to exile the other to the common room just so one of them could have sex. That meant no boys were staying over in their dorm room.

The waitress returned with their drinks, and Claudia watched her take a sip. Bianca winced and coughed as the strong liquor burned the back of her throat, and then she laughed.

"You're right. I hate it. I should've gone with wine." She eyed the bourbon glass with a frown, then giggled. Claudia burst out laughing.

"Oh, boy. You're a one-sip Stella, aren't you?"

"I'm a what?" Bianca tried another sip of her drink. She didn't want to waste it, even if she did hate it.

"One-sip Stella. It means you can't hold your liquor, lady."

Bianca took another cringing sip of the bourbon and nodded. "Okay, I'll own up to that. I'm definitely going with wine next time."

Over the next half hour, the two of them drank their bourbons and talked about classes and boys and their plans after graduation.

"So you're off to California?" Claudia asked.

"Yeah, I have a job waiting for me at the aquarium. There's a couple of amazing marine biologists there who want to show me the ropes."

"That's awesome." Claudia waved the waitress over to order two glasses of merlot. "I'm going to MIT. Got the letter yesterday."

"What?" Bianca squeaked in joy. "Oh my God, why didn't you tell me?"

Claudia blushed uncharacteristically. "I don't know. It makes me feel a bit nerdy, you know?"

Bianca nodded in understanding. Claudia was gorgeous, but also smart. She'd always been embarrassed by her intelligence. Bianca had spent the last four years reminding her roommate that having brains was a good thing. Being pretty was nice, but being smart and having a great career—that was better.

The pair of singers on the stage started a new song.

Bianca felt the music ripple around her, and her stomach suddenly cramped. She winced and got to her feet.

"You okay, Bee?" Claudia started to get up. Bianca pushed her friend back down in her chair.

"I'm okay. I'll be right back. I think the bourbon is just working on my empty stomach."

"Okay, but I'll check on you if you're not back in five minutes," Claudia warned.

Bianca gave a little salute and headed for the restrooms. When she saw the agents trying to come after her, she waved them off. She and Claudia weren't stupid. After four years in college, they had a strong girl code. That included rules like *go find your friend if she's too long in the bathroom* and *never leave drinks unattended.*

Once in the bathroom, she headed for the back stall, pitching to her knees just as she reached it. The bourbon came right up, along with the wine. She moaned in misery. She hated being sick like this. Her skin flushed with an uncomfortable fever, and she pressed her palms on the cold bathroom floor as she braced for another heave. The pain was too much.

"Ms. Wells?" Scott called from the bathroom door. "You all right in there?"

"Yeah, I'm just..." She breathed deeply. Now her whole body was shaking uncontrollably. "Just too much bourbon," she finally finished.

"Why don't we take you home?" Scott offered.

Bianca wanted to scream. She just wanted to be left alone for *one damn night*, to be normal like any other girl.

"I said I'm fine!" she snapped, then immediately regretted it. "Sorry, Scott, I'm fine, really." She swallowed down a wave of nausea, knowing he would hear if she dry-heaved into the toilet again.

"Okay, we'll be outside if you need us." Scott closed the bathroom door. Bianca leaned against the wall, staring at the names and numbers scratched into the painted metal as they started to blur. Everything was blurring now. The world took on a fuzzy hue, and her thoughts became cloudy. She toppled over like a rag doll, her lips unable to form the word she desperately wanted to say: *Help!*

Shadows crept in at the edges of her vision as she saw someone looming over her. *Mike? No. Scott? No. Stranger? Yes. Strange man...help.*

The words played like a skipping record over and over in her mind.

Stranger...help.

The man picked her up in his arms and carried her out of the stall. He left her on the floor as she stared helplessly at the ceiling. Blue and white squares patterned the ceiling like a geometrical arrangement of clouds and sky. But that wasn't right. She wasn't outside. She was... Where was she? Her thoughts swirled in her head as a wave of darkness flushed down around her.

Soren stared at his palm, watching a flood of information illuminate the air just above his skin. These hand-connected devices of Korum's design were ingenious. They connected to the central core control systems in place in all Krinar residences. The Krinar used to have advanced devices that were a thousand times smarter than human computers, which were called common data storage facilities, but Korum had compressed that technology into a small chip implanted in a Krinar's hand. It made it easy to work from anywhere, and Soren could gain access to any information he might need, even from the humans' information databases. He'd just finished reading over the draft of his latest report to Arus when a red alert flashed across his palm.

Bianca's heart rate and blood pressure spiked, then dropped dangerously low. Too low to be safe. Something was terribly wrong with his human female. He called up her coordinates, then rushed out the front door of his new home—a manor house he'd purchased this morning in Princeton—and climbed into the small spacecraft waiting for him outside. He tried not to think about what was happening to her, if she was hurt or sick—and what would happen if he couldn't get there in time.

His ship slipped into the sky and headed straight for Bianca. Even though it took only two minutes to reach the bar, those two minutes felt too long. He left his ship on the roof and leaped off, dropping into the alley below just in time to spot a man dragging a large duffel bag across the asphalt toward a waiting car. The headlights of the car flashed on him as he landed, momentarily blinding him. He roared in rage as he caught the scent of Bianca and blood in the air.

"Fuck!" The man saw him and let go of the bag before he stumbled and ran for his life.

Soren wanted to hunt him down, to rip him to pieces and bathe in his blood, but the need to protect Bianca was stronger. He rushed to the bag, ignoring the squeal of tires as the vehicle sped off. He tore the zipper open and found Bianca bent double in the fetal position in the bag, unconscious. He carefully pulled her free of the duffel, cradling her to his chest. His blood still roared in his ears like the tidal waves off the coastlines of his home world.

"Put her down!" someone yelled. Soren spun to face the two Secret Service agents, their weapons drawn.

"You left her alone!" he snarled. "Some human filth was dragging her away in this." He kicked the bag at the man. The canvas duffel bag smacked one of the agents in the chest. They both lowered their weapons but didn't put them away.

"Ambassador Soren, put Ms. Wells down." The other agent's voice was soothing, gentle, but Soren almost laughed. There was no soothing an angry Krinar. Only his charl could ever reach him in this state. "You do your job and find the man who hurt her. I will protect her—she's in my care now."

He tensed and leaped onto the bar's roof and strode toward his ship, Bianca still in his arms. He got inside the spacecraft and sat down on the flat plank seat, which immediately shaped to his body, and laid Bianca on his lap. The sleek silver ship activated its light-refractive panels and vanished to human sight as it took off.

When the ship landed on the front lawn of his home, he carried Bianca inside and set her down on his bed. He stood there, breathing hard as he fought to control his rage at the one who'd tried to kidnap her and the fear that she'd been terribly hurt. She was so fragile, her human life a mere blink of an eye to someone like him, yet that single blink meant everything to him. His affection for her, his feisty charl, swelled tenfold in that moment as he bent over to brush her hair back from her face. Her skin was as pale as alabaster. Whatever was happening, she was getting worse, possibly dying.

"Hang on, little one—I'll take care of you. Just don't let go."

He accessed the central core technology inside his home and sent Driana an emergency message with his location. He needed her help to save Bianca. She would be invaluable because of her familiarity with human biology.

He retrieved a small medical device called a jansha from his closet and waved it over Bianca's face, then worked it down every inch of her body. Soft light illuminated scrapes and cuts on her arms and legs from where she'd been dragged. They left his sheets stained with small splatters of blood. Rage exploded through him again, and his hand that held the jansha trembled. Doubts spiraled through his head. She should be waking up. He was healing her, wasn't he? Krinar healing devices were very effective, unless the damage was deep inside her and progressed too quickly for his small device to fix what was wrong.

"Soren?" Driana stepped into the bedroom a few minutes later. Soren tensed at her intrusion, his focus so intent on Bianca that he was surprised that Driana had made it all the way to his bedroom without him hearing her.

Driana held up her hands in deference as she stepped into the room, but her eyes filled with worry as they settled on Bianca.

"What's wrong?"

"She's not waking up, and the jansha is ineffective. I don't know what to do." Panic began to set in as he moved to the side, giving Driana room to work. He clasped one of Bianca's hands while Driana looked her over.

"What happened?" Driana asked, her gentle tone slightly calming him. "Be specific."

"She was at a bar. I wasn't with her. I was giving her space. But then I was notified that her heart rate and blood pressure had dropped. By the time I found her, someone had shoved her into a bag like trash and was dragging her toward a car."

"Was it the anti-K resistance?" Driana asked, still looking Bianca over. She focused her own jansha on Bianca's stomach.

"Most likely, but I have no proof to that effect." Soren brushed his fingers over Bianca's brow, removing blonde hair from her eyes.

"She's been poisoned." Driana removed a small pill from a container in the pocket of her trousers and slipped it into Bianca's mouth. "This will neutralize it. We created it to neutralize a wide range of human poisons."

"*Poison?*" The word dripped off his lips in equal venom. When he found the man who'd done this, there would be nothing left of him to identify.

"Yes. A lethal dose, most likely administered via an alcoholic beverage. Whoever gave it to her wanted her dead within a few hours." Driana stroked her fingertips down the column of Bianca's throat, and she stirred, softly moaning.

Soren fell to his knees beside the bed, whispering words of comfort to her in his own language, hating every second that she suffered in pain.

"She will be well now, Soren. But the toxin had already spread to her cells. It will take a while for the antidote to extract and neutralize it all. She will need a few days of rest, with plenty of food and water." Driana touched his shoulder gently in support.

"Thank you, Driana. I..." How could he ever repay her for saving his female?

"Take care of her, Soren. Claim her as your charl now, if that is your intention. Make the necessary arrangements before anyone can stop you. She will need our protection. Her own people will not be able to stop the resistance from killing her."

An aching numbness filled his chest as he gazed at Bianca's face. She was so pale, even her soft, dusky lips were bereft of color.

"Will you be all right?" Driana asked.

He answered with a brisk nod, unable to speak. He couldn't let her see the powerlessness he felt at not being able to help his charl. His heart thumped hard as he brushed his knuckles over Bianca's cheek, his hand shaking as he did so.

He waited an hour until her breathing returned to

deep, slow inhalations and then carefully removed her clothes, leaving only her panties. He slipped her into comfortable oversized pajamas he kept at his residence for when he relaxed in the evenings. Most Krinar males slept naked, but he hoped pajamas would make Bianca feel comfortable and warm.

Once she was dressed, he pulled back the covers of the bed and tucked her in. He used his fabricator to destroy the bloody comforter she had lain on and created a new one. He wanted no reminders of what had happened for either of them. But the fear and anxiety he'd felt at the prospect of losing her so soon would likely haunt him for the rest of his long life.

He poured a glass of water and set it on the table by the bed within easy reach before he went and showered. He needed to purge himself of the stink of the alley behind the bar. He scrubbed his flesh and closed his eyes beneath the hot water.

This was not Zaruth. This was not the cage he had been trapped in for three centuries. He was in an open bedroom, with wide windows facing the lovely Earth woods, moonlight playing among the shadows of the trees. He was not a prisoner—he was free. Nothing was suffocating him or drowning him here. He breathed in deeply, letting the tension in his rigid muscles finally fade as he focused his thoughts back on Bianca.

He lifted his palm up and in his head composed a message to Arus, requesting Bianca be given charl status and her name added to the list of charl humans with the United Nations. Once she was on that list, she would be safe from human interference. No more agents, no more life-threatening situations. He would have control over his wayward female. He would protect her, provide for her. Her father, President Wells, would no doubt be furious, but Soren would mend that relationship later, after he'd fully claimed Bianca as his mate and was assured of her safety.

Soren turned off the water and dried himself before he pulled on another pair of pajama pants. If he crawled into bed bare-skinned, he might forget his self-control come morning when she woke. After a moment of indecision, he sent a second message to his offices in DC, alerting them to notify the White House that he was in possession of Hummingbird, as they called Bianca, and that she was safe. He would speak with the White House in the morning, once he was sure she was feeling better and could talk to her father. He ended the message with a final instruction that he was not to be disturbed. His location here, this secondary residence close to Princeton, was known only to a few of his subordinates at the Krinar embassy.

When he finally slipped into bed beside Bianca, he pulled her into the curve of his body and nuzzled her neck. That sweet vanilla scent teased his nostrils, and he inhaled deeply. Her aroma banished his memories of the cage on Zaruth into a deep dark box in his mind.

"You are mine now, *lilana*. I will never let anything happen to you."

———

BIANCA DREAMED OF DARKNESS, OF BURNING GOLD EYES and soft erotic whispers in her ear. These weren't nightmares, not this time. She had given in, surrendered to Soren, and now there was only pleasure, a pleasure so intense it felt like she was dying.

She bolted upright in bed, reaching for the lamp on her nightstand. Her fingers met only thin air. Groggily, she struggled to find the blasted lamp. Her hand knocked something over, and it crashed to the ground.

"Easy, Bianca, easy," a dark, sleepy voice rumbled from beside her.

Every muscle in Bianca's body froze. Her mind buzzed as she struggled to take in the moonlit surroundings. She was not in her dorm room. She wasn't even in the common room. Where the hell was she?

"Oh my God!" She tried to scramble out of bed, but the person beside her pounced, pulling her flat onto her back beneath him, trapping her with the weight of his muscled body.

Soren.

He gazed down at her, gold eyes swirling with turbulent emotions. He seemed to be searching for something in her face.

"You are safe. You are well. Please, *lilana*, you must rest."

"Soren? What happened? Where am I? What the hell are you doing on top of me?" She bucked her hips, trying to dislodge him, but all she managed was to make it easier for him to settle deeper into the cradle of her thighs. His body responded as any man's would. She felt the press of a large erection, but he made no move to take advantage of her...yet.

"Please, *get off me*," she demanded.

"Only if you promise to stay in bed. You don't realize how close you came to death tonight."

She had been ready to punch him in the face to escape, but his words stilled her. When he rolled off her, she didn't move.

"I... What?" She touched her temples with her fingertips, trying to think of the last thing she could remember happening. She and Claudia. The bar. The terrible bourbon. The bathroom...

"Observe." Soren placed a flat white object on his palm, and it suddenly projected a holographic display in front of her. The image was so clear that when she took in what she was seeing, her stomach knotted with cramps and fresh terror.

A man, whose face was covered with a ski mask,

was dragging her body through the bathroom window. She fell to the ground with a sickening crunch, but the man didn't seem to care. He hauled her through the alley and retrieved a duffel bag from his car, stuffed her into it, and zipped it up.

Bianca touched her throat, imagining how she must have been suffocating in that bag. Then Soren entered the hologram, dropping from the sky like an avenging angel. She watched him rescue her, bearing her in his arms as he faced off with her security detail before he leaped into the sky and disappeared. The hologram faded.

"I retrieved this footage from Krinar monitoring systems placed near the bar you were at last night. You were poisoned. One of your drinks from the bar was laced with a lethal dose of arsenic," Soren said. "Driana, the professor you met yesterday during the campus tour, came here and saved you. You will be all right, little one." He reached for her, and this time she was too stunned to push him away. He shifted her so that she sat on his lap, and he leaned back against the headboard of the bed. He ran a hand up and down her back, whispering soothing words in his own language, one that she had always thought to be rough and unattractive, but right then it sounded like the most beautiful thing in the world.

"You saved me," she finally said.

Maybe it was the fact that she had almost died, or

maybe it was the spell of his eyes and the way they made her think of gold wheat waving in the wind, but she stopped fighting herself and the desire for him that she had tried to bury.

Would it really be world-ending if she kissed him one more time?

She leaned in, tilting her face up to his. His eyebrows rose. He seemed surprised, but she didn't stop moving toward him until their lips brushed together. A tingling in her stomach swept into a swirl of butterflies as her lips moved back over his, coaxing him to respond. She curled her arms around his neck, scraping her nails against his skin, and he moaned in frustration.

"I fear you're not thinking clearly, Bianca. It's the adrenaline and the aftermath. You're desiring physical closeness because you nearly died. We can't do this now." But Soren's eyes were full of bedroom heat that made her toes curl.

"Screw that. I want you, Soren." She stroked her fingertips along a jaw that could have been carved of marble. His thick sooty lashes dipped down as he closed his eyes in pleasure at her caress.

"You don't want this...not yet," he managed to say as he lowered his forehead to hers, their breath mingling together.

"*Now* you're being noble? What happened to the aggressive Krinar male who took what he wanted in the library? Just kiss me," she pleaded. Only his mouth would take away the memories of her brush with death, at least for a little while. He was right about her mental state—she was clinging to him because of the trauma—but it wasn't just that. It was more, had always been more, from that first moment they'd met five years ago. Now she had an excuse to do something completely insane, like this.

"You'll be angry when you come to your senses, Bianca. I won't take advantage, no matter how tempting you are" His hands smoothed her hair back from her face as he put some distance between them.

Damn him and his infernal self-control. She wanted the wildness she'd tasted in the library, that raw hunger that had no limits. She wanted him to take her now in every way possible, because she was too afraid to let rational thought return. If he was the big, bad, sexy alien ravishing a human woman, she couldn't feel guilty for how much she enjoyed it.

He tried to slide off her, but she wrapped her legs around his waist, holding him to her. His shaft pressed against her belly, hard and long and more than a little intimidating, which was all the more reason she didn't want to slow down and let her brain catch up to what her body wanted. She growled at him, hating how he made her burn only to shut her down.

"Shut up and kiss me, Soren," she snapped. Then she moved her mouth to his neck and bit him. She had heard rumors over the years that biting a Krinar male made him lose control.

She was suddenly flipped onto her back, and the aroused Krinar mounted her, pinning her to the downy-soft comforter. His mouth devoured hers, his lips rough and his tongue delving between hers, taking her for his own.

There...*there* was her savage conquering lover from the stars. This was what she wanted, to let him take her so she could surrender to whatever came next without guilt.

Her body was electrified by the connection of their mouths, and soon she was so lost she almost didn't hear the sound of fabric ripping or feel the cool air caressing her skin. Delicious shivers ran through her as Soren's mouth moved down to her throat, then to her collarbone. He nibbled at her skin until she giggled. But her laughter turned into a gasp as he fastened his mouth around one sensitive nipple. Her back arched off the bed as she pressed against him.

Bianca's head swam in dizzying circles as he suddenly sank his teeth into her neck. The sharp pain faded within seconds, and it was like she'd taken a shot of that bourbon straight to the heart. She clutched his head, her fingers tangling in his silky russet strands. Everything winked in and out, like the flashing slides of an old home movie playing through a broken projector.

"Soren..." She whimpered his name as something hard and hot speared into her womb. Pain blurred with pleasure as she felt his cock slam into her. It felt so good, the fullness...the connection between them as he sank deeply into her. There was no end to her, no end to him. He moved slow and hard, crafting a symphony of moans from her lips, torturing her with an aching emptiness and blissful stretches as they came back together again, over and over.

"I'm sorry, *lilana*. Sorry to hurt you this first time. Never again." Soren's words blended together in her head and heart. She would be frightened of him and what those words promised tomorrow, but right now she couldn't think past the flashing points of light in her mind. Soren was finally claiming her in the way she'd dreamed about these last few years, and it was infinitely better than she'd ever imagined.

"Don't hate me tomorrow, *lilana*," Soren murmured in her ear. "I will give you galaxies. I will harness the stars upon your command."

Hate him? How could she hate him? He had saved her. He'd given her this sweet erotic bliss, letting her forget all her fears and worries. Right now, there was only *this*.

Her eyelids grew heavy, and she soon drifted away upon silken dreams of galaxies hanging from shining necklaces and stars trapped in dark-blue velvet boxes.

5

____

Soren watched the morning light move over Bianca's naked body. She lay stretched out on her stomach like a starfish, her limbs reaching for the farthest corners of the bed. At some point, she had kicked her sheets off. He ran a fingertip along her calf and up her thigh, watching her skin break out in goosebumps even as she slept. He mentally connected to the home's thermostat to raise the temperature so she wouldn't be cold.

His chest ached with a cottony warmth he had never experienced before, and it had nothing to do with her blood still humming in his body. He had bitten her, knowing his saliva would stimulate her arousal even further, overwhelming her with pleasure. It had prevented her from feeling the burn of his invasion into her body. He'd known she was a virgin, of course. But he had never taken a lover quite like that before. Untried, so easy to wound. He had hated the cry of pain he'd heard, but he'd done his best to take that pain away. Afterward, he had used the jansha to heal her, so she would feel less sore when she woke.

"Soren…" She whispered his name, drawing his focus away from the curve of her hips. She faced away from him, and when he leaned over he saw her eyes were closed. She was still asleep, and dreaming of him? *Interesting…* He grinned and pressed a kiss to her bare shoulder.

"Next time, I will do much better. You will know such pleasure you will fear it might kill you." He climbed out of the bed and pulled on a pair of trousers before he headed to his office. He sat down at his desk and pulled up his tablet. There was a message from Arus to contact him at once. He initiated the call.

"Arus?" His friend's face appeared in the air as a hologram.

"Soren, I've been trying to reach you for the last few hours. You had your communications turned off."

"I'm sorry," Soren said. "I didn't wish to be disturbed."

Arus noted his bare chest and the faint red scratches where she'd clawed him at the height of passion.

"It seems I'm too late," Arus muttered.

"Too late?"

"You claimed President Wells's daughter," Arus stated, his gaze weary.

"I did." Soren was unapologetic. From the moment he'd kissed Bianca in the library, he had known last night was inevitable.

Arus blew out a frustrated breath. "The president is one of the humans' most important leaders. Everyone is looking for her after you abducted her."

"I rescued her," Soren corrected.

"Do not use semantics on me. I heard what happened. You rescued her and *then* abducted her. Wells is raging in his office right now."

"Her safety was at risk, and her security team was inadequate."

"And you left no information as to where you were taking her or how you could be contacted. I just went to your home in DC, but you weren't there. Where are you? I'm having you located right now if you don't tell me."

Soren looked away. He'd bought this residence for the sole purpose of having a private place away from politics so he could court Bianca properly. Not even his brother, Sef, knew the location of this house. He'd taken precautions to keep his purchase of the house completely under the radar of his own people.

"You can't take her from me, Arus. It's too late. I have tasted her blood, mated her with my bite, and claimed her body. But she will be cared for and want for nothing."

Arus growled. "Try explaining that to President Wells. You took his virgin daughter and drank from her while claiming her body. He will see it as an act of war. The resistance will use this against us in their propaganda campaign. What were you thinking?"

Soren stared at his old friend until he was ready to answer. "I was thinking that I finally found a companion, a true one." He couldn't put into words how much Bianca meant to him now that he'd claimed her. She wasn't just beautiful—she was brilliant and compassionate and brave. She would make him a better Krinar male.

Arus's frown deepened. "I'm sending Sef. He will retrieve the girl and take her home, and you will return to DC, where you and I will meet with the Council."

"Don't send Sef. He will only frighten her." Soren's twin brother didn't trust humans. As a guardian, he had seen the devastation humans caused with their violence. He would not understand Bianca's fear or how she responded with stubbornness when she was afraid.

"Sef *will* be coming. I must go and put President Wells at ease and let him know his child is safe. The message he received from your office was that she'd been drugged and an abduction had been attempted. He won't be calm until he sees her safe and healthy.

Soren, you will think on your decision while you wait for your brother." The image vanished.

Soren had not been chastised like this since he was a hundred years old. Krinar grew to physical maturity at around age twenty-five, same as humans, but they were considered children in society until they reached one hundred. But Arus was right. He couldn't keep Bianca. For now, he had to let her go home and see her father. He could come to her in a few days, once everyone had calmed their tempers.

But he would not apologize for taking her away and saving her life, not even if Arus commanded him to. He rubbed his palm over his jaw, sighing heavily, then rose and returned to his bedroom. If he had only a short time left with Bianca, he wanted to make sure he didn't waste it.

———

BIANCA GIGGLED AND SIGHED AS SOMETHING TICKLED her feet. She kicked out, trying to stop whatever was happening, and opened her eyes with a frustrated huff. A second later she sucked in a breath as she stared into Soren's eyes...and then she glanced down at his half-naked body. He stood at the foot of the bed, the light accenting the play of muscles on his stomach and his perfect pectorals. It was as though he'd been created in a lab, designed for every woman's deepest, darkest, naughtiest fantasy.

"Morning, *lilana*." His sensual mouth curved in a sexy grin that made her womb clench. She wanted that mouth back on her body. She wanted to feel those smiling lips against hers. There was something so decadent and joyful about kissing someone as they smiled, and she wanted to experience that with him.

"Morning," she echoed, still strangely shy of him despite the desire heating her insides like a newborn star.

The light illuminated the russet of his hair as he crawled up the bed toward her, scattering the white pillows in front of him like a tiger pawing things out of its way.

He stopped as he caged her beneath him. She stared up into his tawny eyes, her heart racing and her blood humming with desire—a longing she knew she shouldn't have. But it didn't go away; it only grew stronger as their gazes locked.

"Do you remember last night?" His husky whisper sent shivers across her skin. His eyes caressed her, stroking down her face and neck with invisible fingers. She was torn between embarrassment and desire at the approval he showed of her nakedness.

She struggled to bring the fuzzy memories back into focus. "I..." Their bodies on the bed, him inside her, the soft moans and wicked growls, her screams of pleasure. She reached up to her neck. The skin there was smooth, but she distinctly remembered the pain of him biting her, followed by blinding ecstasy.

"You bit me..." She wasn't accusing—she was more shocked. Krinar *really* did bite during sex? Was it also true they drank blood? She hadn't wanted to believe it was true because the idea was scary as hell. What if he drank too much? Could they do that? Could they drain a human like a vampire?

"I didn't mean to bite you," he said, his tone soft, as though he was able to read her troubled thoughts. "When you bit me, it set off my instincts. You must not do that again, not unless you want me to lose control." He brushed his nose against hers before pressing his tender lips to her own.

The kiss was slow and erotic in a way she'd never imagined. His tongue traced the seam of her lips, seeking entrance. She opened to him, and he swept inside, his tongue playing with hers before he thrust it in and out in a pattern that mimicked what he'd done last night. Her channel clenched, and she clamped her thighs together as a rush of wet heat dampened her panties. She reached up to his face, touching his jaw, which was lined with morning stubble. It rasped against her palms, and she moaned in delight as he deepened the kiss even further.

God, the man could make love with just his mouth. It was the most amazing thing she'd ever experienced.

Threading her fingers into his hair, she marveled at its silky texture as it flowed between her fingertips.

"Are you in pain? Anywhere at all?" Soren asked between kisses. Kisses that she should have hated but didn't. They hypnotized her, made her feel like it was only the two of them in the universe. It was a little frightening and incredibly exciting to feel that way, to be the center of Soren's world.

This is why you never dated anyone seriously, the voice in the back of her mind whispered. *You wanted to feel this way, and you knew only Soren would ever give it to you.*

"I'm not in pain," she promised him before she surrendered to the lazy, sensual hunger rolling through her and kissed him back.

"Good. You must tell me if I ever hurt you. I don't ever want to hurt you, Bianca."

She believed him. His brooding, otherworldly intensity aside, there was only truth in his eyes as he said that.

"I trust you," she whispered. "Can we...can we do it again?" She didn't want to say *make love* or *fuck*. Neither of those expressions seemed to fit what had happened between them. They simply weren't powerful enough.

"You want to?" She saw the heat in his gaze and how he struggled to control himself enough to gauge her honesty.

"Yes. I'm clearheaded. I swear." *As clearheaded as I*

can be when surrounded by this glorious male body, she silently added.

He still seemed hesitant. "If you're really sure."

With a groan of frustration, she slid one hand down his back, beneath the waistband of his pajama pants, and wrapped her hand around his cock and gave it a slow stroke. His eyes rolled back in his head.

"I'm *really* sure," she said with a chuckle, but it died quickly when his focus shot back to her face and he growled softly, his eyes glowing gold.

"Woman, you tempt me like no other." It was her only warning.

He flipped her onto her stomach and tugged his pajama bottoms off. The cold air teased her skin, but she had only a moment to miss the heat of his body before he covered her again from behind. He lifted her hips up, placing a pillow beneath them, which left her ass up in the air. She wriggled, not entirely sure she liked this exposed feeling, but a second later he was right behind her, one hand guiding his cock to her entrance. His other hand dug into her hip, holding her in place as he thrust inside her.

"Oh God!" She squeaked in surprise at the sudden fullness. It was like no part of her was left untouched, unclaimed by him as he sank inside her.

"Does it hurt?" he asked gruffly as he started to withdraw.

"No...it's just...oh my God, you're huge!" She buried

her face in the pillow, stifling a cry of pleasure as he penetrated her again, seemingly even deeper.

"You're so tight, *lilana*, so very tight." He leaned over her, bracing one arm next to her left shoulder as he started a steady thrusting rhythm.

There was no way to describe the feel of him behind and above her, his skin sliding over hers as he merged with her over and over. His hard body above, soft downy blankets beneath, it was the sweetest nirvana she'd ever experienced, and she knew she would never get enough of it...or of him.

He whispered sweet naughty words to her that made her blush and whimper in delight as he told her all of the wicked things he wanted to do to her. The positions he would use to claim her, the places he would take her and then fuck her senseless with everyone nearby completely unaware. All of it turned her on so hard that her channel actually hurt with need.

Bianca screamed his name as she finally came, and she swore she saw the very galaxies he had promised her swirling behind the backs of her eyelids. As she drifted down from that delirious high, he continued to ram inside her, the bed shaking as he used her for his own pleasure, and she loved every intense second of it. His roar shook the room, and he dug his fingers into her hips, holding her beneath him as he emptied himself inside her.

"Holy fuck," she groaned. "I think you broke me." She laughed, but he carefully shifted her so she lay on her back beside him.

"Do you need medical attention?" He ran gentle hands down her body, searching for injuries.

"No, I'm good. Really good. I just meant...*wow*... that was like..." She blushed and covered her face with her hands. He pried them away, his golden eyes changing back to that rich shade of brown again.

"I promised never to hurt you," he said.

"I know. You didn't." She yawned and stretched, her body languid and relaxed. If he was like that all the time, she'd never leave his bed again. She cuddled into his side, trying not to think about the future or what would happen even one hour from now. She knew this would be difficult, that there would be consequences, but right now she wanted to have this moment with him and luxuriate in it for as long as she could.

Soren nuzzled her cheek and placed a tender kiss to her lips, then wrapped her up in his arms, cocooning her with his body. It felt so good to be held, to feel that connection beyond sex. Yet it was scary as well. A girl could get addicted to this.

She had just started to drift to sleep when he sat up abruptly. His attention suddenly focused on the bedroom door.

"I'm here." A deep masculine voice that wasn't Soren's came from behind the closed door.

"Soren, who is that?"

Soren pulled the covers over her, hiding her naked body. Then he pulled on a pair of pajama pants before he approached the door like he had to face a fire-breathing dragon on the other side.

"It's my brother," Soren told her as he opened the door a crack. From where she sat on the bed, Bianca couldn't see anyone on the other side.

Brother? Oh God, this couldn't get any worse or more humiliating.

6

The two Krinar spoke in soft tones, their words foreign to her. Soren retrieved his fabricator from the nightstand and used it to produce a set of fresh clothes for her: jeans, a T-shirt, socks, shoes, as well as a bra and panties. He handed them to her and nodded toward the large marble bathroom without a word. Bianca snatched the clothes and rushed inside the bathroom to get dressed, wishing she could understand whatever Soren and his brother were saying. She'd had no idea Soren had a sibling. Most Ks didn't have a lot of siblings; many were only children in order to control their population.

When she finished dressing, she found the two of them in the bedroom staring at each other. They were identical. Two Sorens. It was like something out of her most secret fantasy. Hers wore gray trousers and a black sweater now, and his brother stood there in jeans, biker boots, and a black T-shirt. She examined them a little more, noting that the brother's jaw was slightly wider, his eyes a hint more shadowed, and his body a little larger perhaps, but those differences were so minute that only someone who was familiar with Soren's body, like she was now, could tell them apart.

"Bianca, this is my brother, Sef." Soren didn't take his eyes off him as he spoke. Sef gave her a cool, appraising look and smirked at his brother.

"She's adorable, brother, but you fucked up. The president's daughter? They're talking about sending you home to Krina. *Permanently*."

"What?" Bianca cut off any further arguments. "Soren, we should talk about this. My father"

"You are leaving with me, Ms. Wells," Sef said. A tic worked in Soren's jaw as he met her eyes at last.

"I will not," she said flatly. "He and I need to talk." She pointed to Soren. "Just give us a minute."

Sef shook his head. "My orders were to remove you immediately, before you could bond with each other further." Sef reached for her when she refused to budge.

What happened next was a blur of violence. Soren launched at his brother, but Sef quickly reversed the move. They collided into the wall next to the door in a deafening crash.

"Bathroom now, Bianca!" Soren snarled as he kicked Sef in the stomach. Sef flew back a dozen feet, skidded to a stop, and ran straight back at Soren. Bianca ducked into the bathroom, listening to the crashes, grunts, and shouts in Krinar. She tried to open the small window by the sink, but it wouldn't open, and her hands were slick with sweat. So she searched the bathroom for any kind of weapon and found not a damn thing she could use. She curled up inside the shower, holding her knees as she listened to the brawl continue. When things finally grew silent, she heard heavy breaths as the door opened. Sef stood there, staring down at her.

"You will come with me now." He waved a hand as she climbed to her shaking feet and entered the bedroom. Her hazy, pleasure-tinted memories from last night were destroyed as she saw the destruction. Lamps were shattered, bedposts broken, bedding covered in blood. Soren lay on the floor, unconscious, blood dripping from his chin and nose.

"Oh my God." She tried to run to him, but Sef barked out for her to stop.

"He will be fine. He's merely knocked out. It was the only way I could help you get free of him. Now come."

Bianca followed Sef to the silver spacecraft sitting on the front lawn. "But I didn't want to leave him, not yet. We need to talk about what happened. He didn't hurt me"

Sef snorted. "You don't understand. No one told you." He motioned for her to climb into the spacecraft. Two flat planks filled the interior, and she sat down on one when Sef gestured for her to do so. Then she tensed as it suddenly morphed around her body, forming a comfortable chair. Sef climbed in and sat on the second plank beside her as the silver ceiling of the ship closed over them. She had a thousand questions about the ship, but Soren mattered far more than that.

"No one told me what?"

The ship lifted off and sped away at a fast pace.

"He has claimed you. He has tasted your blood and body. Many of our kind can taste blood and fuck without attachment, but my brother has made the choice that you will be his. *Forever.* Do you know what charls are?"

"Sex slaves?" She knew the term was wrong but wanted to see what he would tell her instead.

"No. Fuck, you humans are obsessed with that propaganda, aren't you?" He shook his head, scowling. "Charls are human companions to Ks, like mates— that's the closest term I can think of that would make sense to you. He has tried to mate you."

"What?" *Mate?* That was terrifying, and yet the thought of spending nights in mindless pleasure with

Soren wasn't as unwelcome to her as it should have been.

"You would never have been free of him, Ms. Wells. You would have gone wherever Soren went, and been with him forever, sharing his bed as his permanent companion, what you humans would call a mate."

"Until I died?"

"Something like that," Sef said. "Your father was informed that Soren abducted you from your protection detail last night. Now it seems he also took your virginity and your blood. He broke your laws, and while it wasn't against ours, we do treat human laws with some modicum of respect, especially with regards to the treatment of unwilling females."

"I..." She drew in a deep, horrified breath. "I *wasn't* unwilling, and he rescued me. Ask him to show you the footage from the alley. Some asshole poisoned me and shoved me in a duffel bag. Soren saved me. He got there before my Secret Service agents could even react."

"It doesn't matter what you *think* happened. Your father is adamant that you will not become a charl, and that is a promise we made to him in order to keep a peaceful relationship between our peoples. Soren's flight of fancy and your human urges are not more important than that. We must have peace." Sef landed the aircraft in a small patch of woods half a mile from her campus.

"Your security team is just ahead. Go with them." He opened the ship's ceiling, and it reminded her a bit of a fighter jet, only all silver and shining like a mirror. She climbed out and saw the familiar SUV in the distance. Mike and Scott caught sight of her and sprinted toward her through the woods. She turned to face Sef again, hating how her stomach knotted. She saw Soren in his every feature, yet she knew it wasn't him.

"When can I see him again?" she asked.

Sef frowned. "Never. Our Council will be meeting to decide his fate. He will likely be ordered to return to Krina for a few thousand years until he has learned proper restraint."

"A few *thousand* years?" She choked on the words.

"It is for the best, Ms. Wells, I assure you. You have a destiny here on Earth. Find a human mate, bear his children, and live a happy life. It will put your father at ease." Sef climbed into his ship, and the second it closed around him, the ship faded from view using a cloaking device. Bianca stared at the space where it had been. A hollowness filled her chest, and her throat burned as she tried to swallow.

For five long years, Soren had been a seductive, frightening presence in the back of her mind. Last night she'd seen the real Soren. Her protector, her rescuer, her lover. She had judged him with a girl's fear and now mourned his loss as a woman.

I didn't get the chance to figure out what was between us.

"Ms. Wells!" Mike and Scott reached her, panting from their run. "Are you okay? We've been losing our fucking minds." Mike looked ready to hug her, and Scott's head fell back as he looked skyward in relief, one hand pressed to his chest.

"I'm fine," she said, finally realizing how scared they must have been. "Seriously, guys. I'm just fine." She paused and spoke again. "Soren saved me. I was dying. That man from the bar, he poisoned me."

Mike's face drained of color, and Scott's shoulders dropped as they both stared at her.

"We vetted everyone in the bar. Especially the bartender," Mike said with a growl. "How the...? Never mind. We'll find out."

"Can I borrow your phone? I need to speak to my dad." Scott handed her his phone. She dialed her dad's private number and waited. He answered a second later.

"Where is she?" he bellowed.

"It's me, Dad. I'm borrowing Scott's phone."

"Jesus, Bianca! Do you have any idea what's happening? I thought you were dead. Did that bastard K touch you? If I ever see that goddamned mother..."

Bianca closed her eyes and waited for her father to stop cursing. It took a while. "Dad, there's a bigger problem. Someone, probably an anti-K terrorist, poisoned me in the bar, even though the agents vetted my location and the employees. But they still got to me. I was in a body bag, Dad. You hear me? If Soren hadn't—"

"Don't say his name," her father warned.

"Tough. *Soren* saved my life. He took me to a safe location and healed me. He didn't have time to wait there and get debriefed following protocol. You owe him, Dad. I owe him my life."

Her father was silent. Only his harsh, angry breaths came over the phone line.

"I'll issue an apology and thank the Ks for their assistance, but that's it. They can't take you from me, Bianca. Do you understand? You are off-limits. I know we can't stop them from taking what they want, but I can stop them from taking you. I won't lose you, not after losing your mother."

His words made her own heart bleed. She knew how much he cared about her and how hard losing her mother had been on him, had been on them both. Bianca would have loved him for his protectiveness at any other moment, but not right now. "Dad—"

"Don't worry. I'm demanding the K Council to send Soren back home."

She wanted to scream. Why was no one listening to what *she* wanted? "What if *I want* Soren to stay here?"

Her father snorted. "Out of the question."

Bianca's hands shook as rage pumped adrenaline

through her system. She hung up and tossed the phone at Scott and started toward their SUV. If no one was going to listen to her, then she would find a way to get to Soren herself. She didn't know if she wanted to be his charl or not, but she did know that things were unresolved between them. They needed to talk, if nothing else.

And maybe...maybe she could steal another kiss. She couldn't help it. The man was a sexual god, and she didn't want to walk away from that, not when he'd saved her life and shown her how good things could be between them. Her life was just that—*hers*. She was not going to let anyone dictate her future.

"Where are we going?" Mike asked as he helped her into the SUV.

"Back to campus," she said absently. She was already starting to make plans. She needed to find a K, one who could help her find Soren and wouldn't balk at getting into trouble. And she knew where she could find one. She needed to get Claudia to find out where an X-club was.

———

RANDALL TURNER STARED DAGGERS AT THE WOMAN facing him.

"You had one fucking job. Kill that little bitch." Tarah Crowley paced in the dim office, the blinds on the small window tightly shut to keep any cameras or Krinar surveillance out.

"The ambassador showed up. He dropped out of the fucking sky. What was I supposed to do? He nearly killed me," Randall hissed at her.

Tarah continued to pace. Her eyes appeared over-large through her thick glasses, and her dark-brown hair was frizzy and streaked with gray. Randall hated this woman. She was a piece of shit, but she paid him well. Still, he wasn't an idiot. He knew she had made her money by embezzling from the small tabloid paper she ran. Her business model was to create stories if she couldn't find a real one to publish.

"You'll have to find another way to get to her," Tarah muttered. "I want that story. *Krinar Ambassador Kills President's Daughter.*" She flashed her hands in the air as though displaying a visible sign.

"You only paid for last night," Randall reminded her.

She turned her cold, dead, brown eyes on him. "I shouldn't have to pay you again, not until I get what I want."

Randall weighed the amount of money he'd been promised against the odds of battling an angry, possessive Krinar.

"Hire someone else." He turned and walked away. No pile of gold was worth fighting the fury he'd seen in that Krinar's eyes. Randall had escaped with his life.

Barely. He knew he wouldn't next time. He wanted to keep his limbs intact, and the best way to do that was to avoid the K who had protected President Wells's daughter.

Tarah cussed and screamed at him, but it didn't matter. He was done with her, and he walked away.

7

———

Soren groaned as he crawled his way back from the pit of unconsciousness. His body ached in a way it hadn't in millennia. Each muscle protested as he struggled to get up from the floor.

What the fuck had happened? He wiped his mouth to stop whatever was dripping from his chin and nose. His hand came away smeared with blood.

Shattered pieces of ceramics, glass, and plaster dust coated the floor, stabbing his legs and feet as he got to his hands and knees. He glanced up and realized he wasn't alone. His twin, Sef, leaned against the open doorway, watching him. A flash of memories raced through him. His brother had kicked his ass.

"You okay?" Sef asked quietly.

"Yes." Soren struggled to his feet. "You were always the stronger fighter."

"And you the better strategist. It's why I never fight fair with you."

"What?

"I wanted to throw you off balance. Once you were worried about her, your emotions overrode your ability to strategize against me in a fight." Sef was unapologetic, even a little smug. As younger males they had fought plenty of times. Half the time Sef won, the rest Soren won.

"Where is Bianca?" He climbed to his feet, leaning on the blood-covered bed while the nanocytes in his body continued to repair his damaged muscles.

"Safe. Away from you."

Soren walked to the bathroom, taking in the lingering scent of her hair and the sickly-sweet scent of her fear. He hated to think of how she must have felt while he and Sef had fought. He splashed water over his face, removing the blood and sweat.

Sef got up and came to the bathroom door. "She doesn't want you, Soren. You overwhelmed her with your bite, and like any human, she surrendered to the pleasure. It doesn't make her your charl, and you can't force her to be. Let her go." His words were soft, and each one cut Soren deeply.

"She said she wanted to stay and talk to me," he argued, realizing he sounded like a foolish young male.

"She only said that to prevent the fight," Sef said. "She and I had time to talk while I took her away. She said she was only trying to buy time to calm us both down. You frightened her and hurt her, Soren. The Council is going to convene in a week to discuss whether you should return to Krina. I have sent them a statement that you should be able to return to Earth in a thousand years."

The sudden falling sensation in his stomach almost made Soren double over.

"Long enough for Bianca to be gone." The words were like ashes upon his lips as he left the bathroom, shoving past his brother. He couldn't believe his own brother was telling him he would have to just sit and wait while his charl died of old age. It was unthinkable.

"It's for the best. You're eight thousand years old, Soren. You can't be seen losing your head over a human girl. If you wanted a human female, you should have chosen another. I understand how addictive their blood is."

It wasn't about the blood. Yes, the Krinar had evolved into blood drinking out of a biological necessity to replace a hemoglobin in their system due to a deficiency, but they'd developed suitable synthetic blood to drink as needed in addition to their normal food. Biting Bianca had been about reducing the pain of taking her virginity, not blood. She had been so lost in pleasure that whatever pain he had caused entering her had vanished.

"Leave me alone, Sef." Soren prowled toward the

wreckage of his bed and sat down. His body was almost fully healed, but his chest ached, and it had nothing to do with the beating his brother had given him.

"Arus called the president. You will be taking a leave of absence from your position until the Council deals with you. You are to return to your DC residence. Tonight."

Soren stared into Sef's dark-brown eyes. They rarely turned gold because Sef was so used to controlling himself. He had to be—he was one of his people's top guardians. Soren stared hard at his brother, tempted to tell him to fuck off, as a human would so bluntly put it.

Sef read his brother's rebellious intentions. "You will do as Arus commands or face summary judgment from the Council. Is that understood?" He then turned to walk away.

Soren didn't like to part from his twin like this, with dark scowls and angry words, but a wedge lay between them now. Sef had taken his mate, his charl. It was unforgivable. The silence of his anger clouded him as his brother left the house.

Then he stood and began to clean up the remains of the home he'd worked so hard to prepare for Bianca. She'd never even had the chance to stay here except for one night. His thoughts raced wildly. He had to find her, talk to her. If she didn't want him, as Sef said, he would return home to Krina. But if she did want him, he would steal her away, take her somewhere his people could not follow. He knew of one person who could help them with that, one person who would understand. Korum. The male Krinar was one of their people's best technology engineers, but more importantly, he had fallen in love with a human, so much that he'd married her in the human way. He'd proven that devotion to a human and the publicity around such a match could be a good thing. Soren went to his office and contacted him.

Korum's face hovered in the air. "Soren, what can I do for you?"

Soren explained what had transpired between him and Bianca. Korum listened solemnly. He and his mate, Mia, had faced similar challenges to be together.

"What can I do to help?" Korum asked.

"I need to find Bianca and meet with her without being tracked or viewed. I know we have cameras almost everywhere. Do you have any way to hide my presence from them?"

Korum was silent for a moment. "I normally wouldn't give anyone this technology—it's so easily used the wrong way. But I believe you won't abuse it. I have a personal cloaking device, two of them, which are paired together. As long as you and your charl both wear them, it renders you invisible to human eyes and to our monitoring and tracking systems, but you can still see each other."

"That would be good," Soren said, already planning how to find Bianca.

"Here are the schematics. Use them on your fabricator and then delete the designs immediately."

"I will." Soren thanked Korum and ended their communication. He uploaded the files to his fabricator and created the cloaking devices. Two silver bracelets appeared. He slipped his on, pressing a small groove on the side. A sudden shiver rippled along his skin as the device began to work.

Soren grinned, feeling the tightness in his chest ease. He would go to Bianca tonight, steal her away, and claim her again. Her father and the Council be damned. She was his charl, his beloved, and he would not give her up unless she told him to. But he needed to hear that from her lips and no one else's.

"I'm coming for you, *lilana*," he said and closed his eyes, imagining just what he would do once he had her back in his arms and in his bed.

———

"This is a bad idea," Claudia hissed as she trailed behind Bianca.

Bianca wasn't really listening. She was too focused on the crowded entrance to the X-club. It had taken quite a bit of convincing for Claudia's sister's friend to tell them the location of the Krinar nightclub she'd been to. Bianca had figured out how to disable the tracking bracelet and panic button on her wrist thanks to a clever computer engineering student Claudia knew. Mike and Scott would think she was still there, would never know she'd slipped out the back entrance opposite where they watched from their SUV. If she had any chance of finding Soren, it would have to be by herself.

"Okay, I'm scared—I'll just own it," Claudia said as they got in line for the club. Half a dozen scantily dressed women got turned away at the door, so Bianca and Claudia were only a few people from the entrance now. There didn't seem to be any bouncer, but some kind of scanner at the door read each person's face before turning red or green. It turned green for the next person in line, and the door opened just long enough to admit one person before it closed again.

"No one will hurt you," Bianca whispered as she and Claudia reached the door. She hoped that was true. The rumors that Ks took the humans they wanted and made them charls had too much of a ring of truth to be completely discounted.

"You go first." Claudia nudged her forward. Bianca

tried to act confident, but deep down she was shaking with nerves. She looked into the face scanner, and a quick flash of light blinded her a moment before the screen flashed green. The door opened, and she ducked inside. The hall was dark except for the red and blue lights glowing from the floor in slow, rhythmic patterns. She followed the lights and paused as she reached the real entrance to the club.

"Wow..." Claudia came up behind her, leaning against her for support as they stared at the scene before them.

The most beautiful Krinar they'd ever seen were dancing with each other and some humans in sensual patterns on a large dance floor. Fog drifted along the floors and lights, making patterns in the air. Pulsating electronic dance music filled the room, not too loud, but enough that it made her chest vibrate with the bass beats. A bar on the far right had three Krinar males who were serving drinks to a crowd of Ks and humans around a long row of barstools. But there were no rows of human alcohol bottles lining the bar wall like she expected. Instead, the drinks they served were colorful to the point of being fluorescent, served in pretty, slender, tube-shaped glasses.

"So what's your plan?" Claudia asked, and then she perked up with interest as a K passed by them with a tray of cocktails. She took one and sniffed it like a scientist would, attempting to waft it toward her nose with her hand.

"Better taste this first since you're a lightweight." Then she took a sip.

"Well? Too strong?" Bianca asked, watching her with a little smile.

"Not much alcohol. Mostly some kind of sweet fruit juice. It's good—try some. So, Soren. How do we find him?" Claudia asked.

"We don't," Bianca said. Her heart was hammering as she pointed to the dance floor. "I think he found me." There in the midst of the crowd stood the man who'd haunted her dreams. He wore jeans and a black T-shirt, looking more like his brother, but his hair was shorter than Sef's, and those brown eyes were now swirling gold as he caught sight of her. Somehow he had found her. Yesterday that would have scared her, but after what had happened between them, she wanted to run to him and bury her face in his neck and get drunk on the sweet scent of his dark aroma.

Claudia intruded on her thoughts. "Okay, you found your K. What should I do, other than be a third wheel?"

"Whatever you want." Bianca walked toward Soren as though in a dream.

She longed to touch him again, kiss him again, and this time there would be no going back. She could see that in his eyes. They would be on the run together, from his people and hers, and she was fine with that. She licked her lips, and soon she and Soren were only a foot apart. His hands were in his pockets, and he looked oddly relaxed. She was breathless, and her heart wouldn't stop pounding against her ribs.

"Tell me now if what Sef told me is true. Do you want me to leave you alone? This is your last chance to be free of me," he said. Despite the music all around them, she heard his softly spoken words. She didn't know how to respond. She wasn't sure if she wanted freedom or captivity—she only knew she wanted to be his.

"You won't cage me up? You won't take away who I am?" she asked. That was her true fear, that by becoming his, she, the woman Bianca was, would disappear.

His golden gaze softened, and her heart fluttered in response. "Take away who you are? Never. Who you are is what I crave. Your body and your mind matter to me. I want to be the only male in your life, for the rest of forever. That is how I will own you, by giving you endless pleasure."

"And do I own you back? No other women for you? Human or Krinar?"

He nodded without hesitation. "Of course. How could it be otherwise?" She sought out any hint of hesitation or deception on his face but found none.

This was it. There was no going back. She wasn't

going to let her father dictate her life. She wanted the right to choose, and she chose Soren.

"Then yes, I want to be with you." She met his gaze as he slowly reached for her hand, but when she expected him to grasp it, he instead slipped a small silver cuff around her wrist. A strange tingle rippled through her body.

"Soren, what was that? What did you do to me?"

He curled an arm around her waist and pulled her flush against his body so he could whisper in her ear. "I've made you invisible. No one, not my people or yours, will be able to find us unless we wish it." He guided her finger to a small grooved spot. "So long as you are wearing this and you press this button, no one will see you. Press it a second time and you'll be visible again. Mine is tuned to the same frequency so that we can always see each other."

He cupped her face and brushed the pad of his thumb over her lips. A wave of excitement and arousal flooded her at the thought that no one here could see them.

"This is amazing," she breathed. "We won't have to worry about the agents or anybody."

He nodded, smiling down at her. "It will only be us, *lilana*," he promised. Something about the way he said that made her tremble with excitement. She and Soren now had a chance to be alone, and she knew what she wanted. She bit her lip and slipped her hand into his.

"This way, little one." Soren led her away from the dance floor. She looked back, only to see Claudia talking to an attractive Krinar male by the bar. She seemed safe enough. Then Bianca followed Soren into the darkness.

As they descended into another lower level, she shivered with apprehension. The walls pulsed with colors, and the sounds and scents of sex were all around them. Soren pressed his hand to one of the walls, and it melted away in the air. Then he pulled her into the room with him. There was a circular bed that floated above the ground.

"Oh my God." She stared at the bed, fascinated. Lucy had been telling the truth about the floating furniture after all. "How?"

"A simple gravitational field." Soren touched the wall beside the vanished door, and it rematerialized, sealing them inside. Then he faced her, his eyes glowing in the dark, the soft neon colors of the glowing walls reflected in his eyes. He stepped toward her, and she took a step back, but her legs hit the bed and she fell back, landing on the bed. He kicked off his boots, pulled his shirt over his head, and unbuttoned the single button above his zipper on his pants, but he left them on. The prospect of doing that for him was intensely erotic. It made her think he was going to take his time with her, but the second he couldn't hold back, he'd rip those pants down to be inside her.

"No more running. You're mine," he growled. The wolfish gleam in his alien eyes made her shiver with awareness. She was his, yes, but for some insane reason she didn't want to make it easy for him. She needed him to be wild, to be on the hunt, to demand her submission.

"Prove it," she growled back in open challenge.

Surprise flashed across his eyes, then a primal hunger heated his gaze, and he lunged for her. She got onto her hands and knees, scrambling away from him. She made it only two feet before he trapped her against the wall. He didn't hurt her, but there was no way she could get free. He fisted a hand in her hair, baring her neck so he could press kisses against her skin over the spot he'd bitten last night.

God, she wanted him to bite her again, but being pinned against the wall made that impossible. She bucked her hips, which only ground her ass against his groin harder. She could feel the thick, impressive bulge of his shaft through his jeans. Soren pressed his teeth into her shoulder, not piercing the skin, but holding her in place like a tiger with its mate while he slid his free hand up her inner right thigh to cup her mound.

He pushed her panties aside, slipping one finger into her and growling as he found the wetness inside. She continued to fight, trying to urge him to take over completely, to own her body in the way she now craved. He pinched the sensitive bud of her clit, and she squealed as a mixture of pleasure and slight pain blurred her thoughts. He shoved her dress up over her hips and slapped her ass hard. Then he tugged her underwear down to her thighs, leaving her exposed. She shivered and writhed, her belly clenching as she took the pleasure he gave her and pushed against him, wanting more. Every cell in her body stilled as she heard the zipper of his jeans.

Without any warning, he pulled her hips out and thrust up inside her. She gasped and arched on her tiptoes, surprised by the sudden fullness. She turned her head to the side more as he kissed her. It blew her mind how he could kiss her while fucking her hard against the wall like this. Her legs buckled, but he held her up, filling her, making the pleasure build in steady yet almost violent waves as he took her. Blood throbbed in her veins, and she closed her eyes, absorbing every delicious sensation of his body and hers, spinning them deeper and deeper into a web of erotic desire.

The heat of his hard chest pressed to her back, and his warm breath mixed with hers as their lips separated for a moment, sending her spiraling higher. Mindless ecstasy captured her, and she was lost in the throes of an orgasm so powerful she couldn't even make a sound. She went limp as he thrust into her a few more times, and then she felt a wave of heat inside her as he came, which she welcomed with a heavy, contented sigh.

"*Lilana,*" he purred as he withdrew from her and scooped her into his arms. He placed her tenderly on the bed, his masculine hands brushing the hair back from her face before she was stripped of what remained of her clothes. She stretched out like a sacrifice to a pagan god and loved every moment of it, loved seeing her K lover gaze down at her with open lust.

"My *lilana,*" he repeated, then crawled up her body, trapping her beneath him. This time when he entered her it was slow and gentle, but each thrust was deliberate, as was each kiss on her cheeks, her closed eyelids, the tip of her chin, nose, and lips. Each time he kissed her and thrust into her, he whispered more sweet words in Krinar. She wished she could understand him.

"Soren..." She breathed his name, too afraid to whisper more than that. Little thrills rippled through her like electric pulses each time he joined his body with hers and every time their lips met. She raised her hips, meeting him with equal vigor. And when she dug her fingers into his shoulders, he growled in approval.

"Yes. Mark me, Bianca. Make me yours." She dug her nails into him harder, holding him close, showing him how much she wanted this, wanted *him*. The climax that came this time was slower, deeper, reaching not just her womb but her guarded heart, which now trembled with an emotion she was afraid of, but it was too late to stop. It was inevitable.

Soren went rigid above her, and at last he did what she'd been hoping he'd do to her all this time. He bent his head to her neck and bit down. She felt a shock of pain, and then it all blurred into endless pleasure. His words faded as she tumbled into ecstasy and oblivion.

"My sweet *lilana.*"

8

Bianca stirred awake beneath gentle touches, feathery kisses, and exploring fingers. Sunlight teased the backs of her eyelids with a heady warmth. She wanted to moan at the sheer delight of so many wonderful sensations she was experiencing.

A deep chuckle only furthered her delight, and she wriggled in the luxurious softness of whatever she lay upon. When she finally focused on the world around her and opened her eyes, she gasped. She and Soren lay on the bed floating in a wood hut above pure blue water.

"Where are we?" she asked in a daze. She noticed the shore was a good fifty feet away. They weren't at the X-club anymore?

Soren cupped her face and brushed his nose against hers. "We're exactly where we should be."

"But we were at the club..." She tried to piece together the scattered remains of her memories from the previous night.

"We fucked until dawn, and then you collapsed in my arms and slept. I carried you to my ship and flew us here."

"Fucked until dawn? Shouldn't I be sore?" She touched her thighs, expecting to wince, but she felt no pain.

Soren lifted a small device and waved it at her.

"What's that?" She wrinkled her nose.

"A jansha. It heals almost anything except major injuries. We have stronger, more advanced devices for emergencies like that."

"I don't know if the idea of you being able to fuck me like that and then wave a magic wand to fix me is scary good or scary bad."

He set the device on the table beside the canopy bed and pulled her closer, their naked bodies sliding against one another. This place was so different than the dark basement room with the circular bed that floated off the floor. That place had been dark, erotic, this place was...sensual and relaxing. Soren knew just how to seduce her.

"I would never truly hurt you," he said, and the soft, earnest tone of his voice stirred her heart.

"Soren, I still don't understand how we got here.

Why me? I mean, I'm just nothing compared to those beautiful Krinar women. I can't understand why"

He silenced her with a blazing kiss. Only when she was breathless and on the verge of forgetting her question did he answer.

"I saw fire inside you when we first met. You were too young then for me to see you as a potential companion, but I saw that fire, that bravery, that belief in protecting your people and fighting against a force you couldn't understand, let alone resist. Females like you don't come along very often in the universe, and it is even rarer in your species. I have never felt this way with any females of my kind. They have been nice to be with, but you? It's like I'm waking up for the first time in my entire life. No other female has ever made me feel alive as you do." He stroked a fingertip down her cheek, his face full of tenderness.

She stared up at him in drowsy delight as he continued to speak.

"You are fragile and have far more to lose and to fear. Yet you challenged me without hesitation, without question. Not with violence or hatred or fear—rather, you responded with brave curiosity. You are the future that mankind should strive to achieve. Sons and daughters of this world should want to explore the stars, not destroy the planet beneath their feet. Life is not about taking what you want at the cost of others or living only for oneself. My people—all good Krinar, at least—believe that their worth is measured by what we do for others. Our greatness is built upon our kindness, our charity, our bravery to do what is right, not what is easy." Soren brushed his elegant fingers along her cheek as she listened to his rich, deep voice, utterly spellbound.

"You really think that I'm good?"

His lips curved in a seductive smile. "Not good. *Amazing.* I know your dreams, little one. You wish to study the seas, to help the animals who live there. You want to protect and preserve the beauty of your planet. There is nothing more noble than that."

She started to smile, but it soon faded. "But I won't be able to do that anymore, will I? Now that we're running away?"

"Oh, *lilana*, have you no faith in me?" He sighed in bemusement and stole a kiss from her lips. "The cuff I gave you will be our secret weapon. I will use mine to come to you and you to me. So I will return you to your dorm in a few hours, and your watchdogs will be none the wiser. You will finish your degree, and then we'll move to the West Coast when you start your job in Monterey Bay. I will be with you in secret, and once it's safe, once everyone is ready to accept us, we will be together in the open. I don't want your life in danger from being seen with me until I'm certain I can fully protect you at all times."

Bianca touched her throat, trying to find the words

to express how happy she was. But she couldn't, so she did the next best thing. She kissed him back.

An hour later, Soren pulled her from the bed and provided her with a pretty swimsuit, navy-blue with polka dots, like something a 1940s pinup girl would wear. He wore navy-blue trunks, and they leaped off the ledge of the hut into the water below to swim and splash about in the shallows.

After they'd had their fun playing in the water, Soren caught her by the waist. She curled her arms around his neck as he carried her to the shore, and then they lay upon the hot sand, soaking up the sun.

"Tell me about you. I don't know anything but your name and that you have a brother." She reached across the white sand and threaded her fingers with his.

His eyes were closed, and she had a moment to study him unobserved, his handsome features, strong chin, sensual lips, straight nose, and enviable dark lashes. For the first time, she understood the power of falling in love and being able to watch someone you cared about and memorize every feature. She would never forget anything about him.

"Sarket, my father, and Sarina, my mother, are about nine thousand years old, which is very old in our society. They still live on Krina, but once we have made Earth safe, they plan to come here. With our sun dying, my people will all eventually have to leave."

"Your sun is dying?" She hadn't heard this before. So much about Krina and the Krinar was kept a secret.

"It is far older than yours. It's an ancient red god that is slowly lying to rest in our sky. It has but a few more million years before it dies and life on Krina will perish without its heat. That's why we have come to Earth. We've been watching over you, careful not to interfere in your evolution too much. But it was time we showed ourselves. We need to establish good relationships with humans so that we can safely transition our population here without violence. We want no bloodshed."

Bianca moved closer and rested her cheek on his shoulder as the warm sun beat down upon their bodies. "Humans are afraid the Krinar will be in control forever, that we'll be nothing more than slaves."

Soren's lips twitched, and he chuckled. "I understand your fears, but the control is necessary for now. In a few hundred years, humans will see that control was to protect them. Once they are comfortable with us and we with them, we will not need to control them. We intend for humans to become our equals someday. You are a young race, making leaps and bounds, but still so very young. Right now, you are your own worst enemies. You must learn to trust us. Great things will come once you do."

She placed a hand on his stomach, feeling his corded muscles twitch beneath her palm.

"So the Ks don't really want to control humans?"

"No, little one, we don't." He looked her way and smirked. "Except, perhaps, in bed. We are far more aggressive than humans." He suddenly rolled and pinned her beneath him in the sand and covered her face with kisses while he trapped her hands on either side of her head. She moaned as her body responded wildly, *hungrily* toward him. His domination of her made her wet and aching.

Their tongues dueled for a long, pleasurable moment before he let go of her hands. They got up, and he carried her back to the hut on the water. After he made love to her, leaving her sated and sleepy from the sun and sex, he simply held her close.

"I know more about you than most people," he murmured. "But all of what I know is from our files on you. Would you tell me what it's like? To be the daughter of the leader of what you call the free world?"

She nuzzled his chest, letting out a sigh as she closed her eyes, and after a moment she spoke.

"I lost my mom when I was young. That was... hard. Dad loved her so much. He isn't like most politicians. He and my mom were childhood sweethearts, and he got into the politics game late. He didn't even want to be president—it just kind of happened. After my mom died from breast cancer, he just fully lost himself in it. But he still loves me. I know how much his work means to him, so I didn't complain about the security details or the charity balls or the political dinners."

Soren rubbed a hand up and down her bare back, soothing her in a way she hadn't realized she needed. It was as though he could tell she'd wanted to talk to someone about this for a long time but had never had the chance until now.

"I understand your father focusing on work to escape the dark oppression of tragedy in his life. You are a good daughter to help him through that grief by being at his side, even when you were grieving your mother's loss too."

She sniffled, her nose suddenly burning as she blinked away tears.

"When you invaded Earth on K-Day, it scared me, Soren. You just showed up, and I never had the chance to deal with it, the feeling of losing my planet, losing my future as I knew it."

"We didn't want to scare you, but we had to be firm, or more lives would have been lost. We couldn't afford to let the nations of Earth attempt to attack us. We had to take control right away."

"I know—I get it. But you scared me too, Soren." She shivered, remembering how he'd caused her nightmares and her sexual fantasies for the last few years.

"I didn't know." He lifted her head, and she looked

up at him through tear-coated lashes. "But I promise you will never need to fear me again."

She managed a smile. "I know. I'm not afraid anymore." She turned her face against his palm so she could press a kiss to his skin, and the soft affection in his eyes warmed her all over.

If only they could stay here on this island and never worry about anything ever again...but that was a foolish dream. They both had important jobs—or at least, they would once she was working in the aquarium to help conservation efforts for the ocean. She wouldn't give up her dreams to be his charl, and if he stayed true to his word, he wouldn't make her give them up.

When they were ready to leave, Bianca bid the beautiful hut on the water farewell. She and Soren climbed into his sleek silver ship on the shimmering white sands of the small private island. Within half an hour, they were back in New Jersey. He landed the ship on the lawn outside her dorm, and she paused at the sight of the agents in their car, still watching the dormitory. They didn't react upon seeing her standing there next to Soren or his alien craft, which the bracelets had also been attuned to. She waved a hand at Mike and Scott, stunned that Soren's cuff really seemed to work.

"Remember, you must press the small groove on

the side to turn off the cloak. But don't do it until you are back in the building."

Bianca turned back to Soren, afraid to let him go. "What... What will you do?"

"For now? I will find a new place to live nearby and will come for you tonight."

"Okay." She pulled him to her for one more kiss. She didn't want to think about how addicted she had become to him in so short a time. A glint of humor lit his eyes as he tapped the tip of her nose with his finger.

"Work hard so tonight I can fuck you for hours and not worry about your exams."

She batted her lashes at him. "You'd better deliver on that promise."

He bent his head to nip her shoulder and cupped her bottom. The feel of his large palm gripping her, squeezing gently, only doubled her arousal. Her body throbbed with a desire for him to bite harder.

"That's a promise I'll keep," he assured her with a wicked wink, then turned back to his ship. Soon it rose into the sky and shot away toward the sun.

Bianca watched the horizon a long moment before she sighed and headed inside her dormitory. He'd left her in a state of sexual frustration, and now she'd have to try to focus on her studying. Claudia was at her desk in their room. When Bianca closed their door, Claudia looked up, eyes wide in panic. She slowly reached for the drawer that held her can of Mace.

"Who's there?"

"Claudia, it's me!" She scrambled to find the groove on the cuff Soren had given her, and then she felt tingling all over her body when she pressed it. Claudia screeched and fell back onto her chair.

"Jesus, Bianca!" Claudia pressed a hand to her chest. "You scared the shit out of me!"

"Sorry."

"You okay? I couldn't find you last night, but I didn't want to call the agents. You looked like you knew what you were doing. We really need a system, you know? Text me next time."

"You're right." Bianca flopped down on her bed, her body languid after her marathon of sex with Soren. Claudia seemed to notice this with a cheeky smile.

"So spill it. What happened?" She sat on her own bed opposite Bianca. "Or should I say, how much happened and how often?"

"We went to that basement room your sister's friend mentioned. It was... Oh my God. I can't even... The furniture actually floats like your sister's friend said. And...he bit me, Claudia." She pulled down her blouse just past her neck, but she knew there were no marks, no evidence of that life-altering bite.

"What was it like?"

"Fucking *amazing*. You can't imagine. He's..." She couldn't believe she was telling a friend about this, but she felt like she needed to tell somebody. "We did it against the wall, and then he bit me, and we did it again in bed until dawn. I only remember bits and pieces. After they bite you, it kind of scatters your mind a bit. I can only see last night like a highlight reel. You kind of lose your mind. And everything they do afterward feels *so good*."

She rolled onto her back and stared up at the ceiling, remembering all the dirty things Soren had done to her, how much she'd loved it—hell, *begged* for it. To go from a virgin to a Krinar sex toy in just a few days should have been shameful, but she couldn't hate herself or Soren for simply embracing who they were together.

"Wow! High-five, girl." Claudia lifted her hand up, and Bianca delivered. Then they both laughed.

"So what about you? Did you stay at the X-club long?"

Claudia's face reddened. "Oh yeah. There was a K there named Magnus. He was working the bar. I waited there for a bit to see if you would come back, and when you didn't, I got to talking to him. Then he took his break, and we danced for a while. It was nice. *Real* nice. I'm going back to see him tonight. He'll be working, but at least he'll be there to spend the night with me." Claudia bit her lip. "Did the bite hurt? I'm afraid that..." She trailed off.

Bianca looked at her friend. "It hurts a little, only for a split second. Then all you feel is pleasure." She paused. "Just be sure you trust him, though. Once you're bitten, you're not really in control anymore. They can do *anything* to you. So make sure you trust him."

Claudia frowned. "Maybe I shouldn't go…"

Bianca had an idea. "I can ask Soren about Magnus, make sure he's a decent guy if you want."

Claudia brightened. "Could you?"

"Absolutely. Now, let's get some homework done. Soren made me promise to work hard, or else no sex tonight."

Claudia snickered. "Girl, you got it bad."

Bianca couldn't disagree. She had it very bad indeed for that sexy Krinar ambassador.

———

SOREN ENTERED HIS HOME IN WASHINGTON, DC, unsurprised to find his twin there waiting for him.

"You were supposed to return here last night. I waited for you." Sef shrugged off his leather motorcycle jacket. Soren stared at the garment in surprise. Their people no longer ate meat or used animals for any purpose such as coats. Yet here his brother was, wearing leather. Sef followed Soren's gaze back to the jacket.

"My latest assignment. The Council wants me to infiltrate a group of resistance fighters in Kansas. I'm going incognito, as the humans would say." Sef grinned. "I have contacts to make my eyes blue, and I'll be dyeing my hair blond. No one will know I'm Krinar. It's primitive, but it should be effective."

"Sounds like you found your calling," Soren muttered.

Sef frowned at him. Neither of them was accustomed to discord between them. They were somewhat unique. Naturally conceived children on Krinar were rare, given their lifespans, and twins were almost unheard of. When they were born, their scientists had run hundreds of tests on them. As they had grown up, their lives had continued to be monitored with interest. Soren and Sef had never shared just how deep their emotional connection ran, that at times they could in fact sense the other's emotions.

When Soren had been captured on Zaruth, Sef had known he was still alive and had spent the next two hundred years trying to find him before the Council had commanded him to stop. They had chosen wisely to push Sef into the role of a guardian, letting him pursue justice for their people since he could not rescue his own brother.

When Soren had returned a hundred years later, he had changed and so had Sef. Darkness shrouded them both in different ways. Soren had grieved the loss of freedom and grieved the loss of his other half. The easy dependency between them had been severed.

Soren often wondered if Sef was secretly still angry with him for disappearing, for leaving him alone when they had made a promise to never do that to one another.

Sef watched him closely, leaning back against the kitchen counter as he sniffed the air. Soren wasn't foolish—he had washed himself twice to erase Bianca's scent from his skin.

"So where were you last night?"

"Grieving the loss of my charl," Soren replied. If he dared to say something more flippant, it wouldn't be true, and Sef would know it.

Sef crossed his arms over his chest, his intense gaze still on Soren. "You're a little old to be pouting, aren't you?"

Soren struck without hesitation, curling his fingers around Sef's throat and smashing his brother into the wall by the fridge. Sef struggled to get free, his eyes finally showing a hint of gold lurking beneath the brown.

"You beat me yesterday. I deserved it for stealing Bianca away and taking her virginity like that. But you will not win the next fight so easily. I suggest you hold your tongue, brother." He gave Sef's throat another squeeze before releasing him. Sef coughed and slapped a hand on the wall behind him for support, but he wasn't angry. There was instead a strange look of relief on his face.

"*There* you are. Been wondering if I'd ever see you again."

"What do you mean?"

"The brother I knew before Zaruth was a fighter. The male who came back from that planet was too cautious, too afraid of life, especially living his own." Sef reached out and clapped his brother's shoulder. "You'll need that fighting spirit when you meet with Arus." Sef left him alone, and Soren waited for the sound of the front door closing before he relaxed. He exhaled slowly and headed into his office.

Several video messages awaited him from Arus, and he played through them all. By the last one, he could see the growing tension in Arus's face. He contacted Arus; it took only a moment for them to be connected.

Arus looked relieved. "You didn't report in last night."

"I'm not exiled yet. My time is my own, for now."

"I was worried you might have done something foolish."

"I needed time to grieve losing my charl, Arus. I'm sorry you couldn't reach me."

Arus's gaze softened. "I can imagine how you suffer. Even having a charl for one day is long enough to feel the pain of losing her."

Soren didn't like to lie to his friend, but the die had been cast. He would do anything to keep Bianca. As long as she wanted him, he would do everything to make her his.

"The Council is still discussing the matter. I am doing my best to convince them not to send you back to Krina. But as you have been removed from the ambassador position, your ranking in society is falling. Many agree you should have chosen more prudently who you wanted as a companion. There are billions of human females to pick from. You did not need to choose the daughter of a leader whose support we need."

Soren nodded as though chastened, but secretly he replayed in his mind the moments of making love to Bianca in the large canopy bed on a private island in the Caribbean. How she'd screamed his name when she'd come undone beneath him. Then he remembered how she'd lain beside him on the sand and held his hand while he'd talked of his family and his people. He would have no connection to another woman the way he did with her. There could be no other. If he had to, he would wait, seduce Bianca over the next fifty years, and when her father died of old age, there would be no one to protest, and Bianca would be his without fear of consequences.

"Arus, do you wish for me to leave the city?" he asked.

"I think it's for the best. I'm going to have you reassigned while we await the Council's decision."

"What about the West Coast? I think putting distance between myself and the president would be wise. There are several conservation movements and organizations I feel I could help."

"Human organizations?" Arus asked curiously.

"Yes. I could reach out and see if they wouldn't mind working with our people. We could do much to help them."

Arus was silent a long moment and then nodded. "I like this idea. I will also report this to the Council. I believe it will help your chances of staying on Earth."

"Thank you, Arus." He meant it. Yes, he was lying to his friend about his intentions, but nothing would keep him from courting Bianca in secret. No one would know. No one would get hurt.

———

Tarah paced the length of her office, scowling as she watched the TV beside her desk. It showed the president touring a shelter that had been recently designed by K technology to provide food to the homeless.

Ambassador Soren always accompanied the president on these quaint little outings, yet the ambassador was conspicuously absent today. The president's daughter was also missing. Tarah knew the girl lived in the Princeton dorms, but she was frequently flown home for official functions. No doubt Tarah's attempt on Bianca's life had left her father more determined to protect her.

"That little bitch is going to die."

Bianca should have been dead. She should've been found outside of an X-club. Her death was supposed to make the Krinar look like the monsters they really were, and Tarah's newspaper would have covered the exclusive story, revealing to the world that the Krinar were killers, not the kind and benevolent overlords they purported themselves to be.

Tarah stared at the TV for a long minute, then picked up a burner phone from her desk and called a number she'd memorized.

"This had better be good," a gruff voice answered.

"I thought you'd like to know that President Wells's daughter has garnered the *special* attention of Ambassador Soren."

There was a long silence, and the man spoke more softly. "And why does this interest me?"

Tarah scowled. "Don't be naive. K males only get interested in women for one reason. To fuck them. Soren has been seen rescuing her, whisking her away to God knows where. She wasn't returned to her home immediately after the attack, not until a *full day* passed. A lot can happen in a day. I think you need to look into it. Consider using her to get to Soren. If he's made her a charl and you capture her, you will have control of one of the most powerful Ks on the planet. You might even be able to make them leave Earth."

Another pause, this one quicker, though.

"Doubtful. But it is leverage, if nothing else. She's still studying at Princeton?"

"Yes. She has a two-agent detail, but they don't go inside her dorm. The way I see it, you find a way in that building or anywhere that she's alone and"

"We'll take it from here." The man cut her off, and the line disconnected.

Tarah smiled for the first time in days. President Wells had made a mockery of her paper, even threatening to investigate her finances, and now... Now she would be able to take away what he loved most. His only child. She would have the added bonus of making the Krinar look guilty. Once Bianca was dead, the president would retaliate, and her paper would make a fortune off the bloody outcome.

"Nobody fucks with me." Tarah laughed softly. "Nobody."

"I'm sorry?" someone said from the doorway to her office. She spun and saw a janitor with a mop staring at her in confusion.

"I—Oh, fuck off!" She dissolved into an angry snarl and slammed the door in the janitor's face.

9

Bianca slipped off her Secret Service alert bracelet and then pressed the small groove on her Krinar stealth cuff, as she'd decided to call it. The flash of tingling on her skin lasted only a few seconds. She went to look in the full-length mirror on the inside of her closet door. She stared at the empty space where her body should have been. She looked down at herself and could still see her body, her black cocktail dress and black heels with the little red bows on the back. But when she looked in the mirror, nothing. This Krinar technology really was amazing.

She slipped out of her dorm and headed toward the sleek silver ship waiting on the front lawn. She could see it, but no one else could. It was hard not to laugh at Soren, who was staring at the agents at their usual location in the SUV. When he turned to face her, his brown eyes burned a honey gold.

"Fuck, Bianca, you look good enough to eat." He pulled her against him and kissed her until she was dizzy and excited.

"Hey." She greeted him with a silly grin, trying not to think about how this man had turned her into a purring cat who craved his affection more than anything in just a few days.

"Hey." He greeted her solemnly, but she saw the flash of teasing in his eyes.

"So, what are we going to do?" she asked.

"We are seeing a ballet in London." He helped her inside the ship, and she sat down on the slender plank, which morphed into a seat around her body. She was still getting used to Krinar technology and couldn't resist wriggling a little to test out the range of motion. Soren chuckled as he piloted the ship. He tapped the colorful screen a few times before he settled back and pulled her chair closer to his. She leaned against him, and they watched the skies darken as they moved higher and higher into the air. Normally, it would take eight hours to fly to London, but it took only an hour and a half in Soren's craft.

"Why don't we teleport, like you did on K-Day?" she asked. It was something she'd been meaning to ask him the last few days as she was getting more comfortable with Krinar technology.

"Ah, I was wondering if you'd ask me that. The device I used to appear in the White House that day was a very special short-range device. It works only within a few miles. We're working to extend the distance and now have it up to fifty miles. The use of the machines is heavily regulated since not all of my people have the self-control needed when using such a device. Being here on Earth, full of its new temptations"—he looked at her with a mischievous wink—"we have to make sure our people learn to obey our laws, which means not using our technology carelessly around humans the way we would at home."

"So the humans can't get it, right?" Bianca frowned at him. "That's not fair, you know. The technology is—"

"Incredibly dangerous. The average human would be tempted to misuse it since the balance of power would be in their favor against other humans. We plan to ease use of our technology into your society in small pieces over time to allow you to adjust."

"Okay, you have me there." She couldn't deny that most humans would definitely misuse alien technology for their own selfish purposes.

"Don't be disappointed. As my charl, you'll be allowed to use the technology when you're with me among my people, or in our home."

She trembled with delight at the thought of a home she'd share with Soren and the future life they would have. *Damn, Claudia was right. I have it bad.*

They landed on a special Krinar airstrip outside of London. She and Soren got into a black cab, which took them to the Royal Opera House in Covent Garden. As they stepped out of the car, a thick fog rolled in, curling around one of the streetlamps, dimming the golden glow. The eerie beauty of a London fog night made Bianca lean into Soren and curl her arm around his. Dozens of people in fine clothes, more than a few of them Ks, wandered up the steps of the opera house, their feet vanishing into the tendrils of the fog.

"I haven't been to London since my father became president," she told Soren.

"It's an amazing city. I admit, I prefer it over DC."

"Then why do you stay in DC?"

He shot her an amused, indulgent look. "Arus actually wanted me to travel to more cities around the world and live in the cities for a few months at a time, but I did not wish to be too far from you. I convinced him that I should stay in DC."

"Because of me? I was just a kid when we met..."

"You were, and I did not think of you as a potential charl then, but I convinced myself it was important to stay close to your father—and therefore you—as part of my duties. That keeping an eye on you was in the best interests of my people because of how important you are to your father. But I confess, I did have a connection to you that first moment I saw you. I recognized your bravery, your need to seek answers but not necessarily fight with violence. You challenged me without outward fear, and that fascinated me. It was only after we met again on the campus tour that I had to face that my curiosity was turning to obsession."

They stopped at the top step to the Royal Opera House, and he cupped her chin in his hand and looked into her eyes. "I have waited eight thousand years to find you, and I have not doubted for one second that you were perfect, and perfect *for me*."

A warm glow built inside her, and she basked in his words and the intimate way he created moments like these, even in the midst of a bustling city.

"It's crazy, you know," she whispered. "To do this." She gripped one of his wrists and brushed her fingers over his skin. He was so warm to the touch. Always deliciously, invitingly warm.

He quirked a brow at her. "To do what?"

"People don't just fall in love this fast. I don't believe in love at first sight."

"Love at first sight? Oh, *lilana*, how you delight me with your human phrases." He chucked her chin like she was an adorable child.

She growled a little, but then she laughed as well. "What I mean is I can't love you, not yet. This feeling has to be lust, doesn't it? Really powerful, mind-blowing-sex-based lust."

"Close your eyes, Bianca," he urged. After a

moment's hesitation, she did.

"Now, let all your thoughts go. Abandon all your focused feelings and simply let your body tell you the truth. Do you want me? Do you want to be with me always?"

Until the end of time. The thought came to her softer than the fog that had wrapped itself around London. If she hadn't pushed away her thoughts and her sensibilities to listen to that quiet little voice, she might never have heard it.

She opened her eyes, feeling calmer now than she had been before. "Yes." Soren trailed a fingertip down her nose and then to her lips.

"I felt that instinct the first moment I kissed you. You are still young. I've had far more practice and know when to listen to it. I knew you'd be afraid of what I am, that you would sense that instinct and it would confuse you. So I waited for you to feel it as I do. I'd planned to woo you slowly, but then you asked me to claim you, and I couldn't say no. I was right about what lies between us." His obvious smugness should not have been so charming, yet it was.

"You know, you're lucky you're a hot alien, or I'd be tempted to slap that smirk off your face." She chuckled and delicately cupped his cheek, giving it a playful but tender slap, which made him laugh. The rich baritone sound made her entire being hum to life like strings plucked on a harp.

She rolled up on her tiptoes and stole a kiss. She savored the feel of his soft lips over hers. She opened for his tongue, and he thrust it inside in slow, seductive patterns that made her flush with heat. He knew just how to make her more eager for his kisses, even in public, and for once she didn't care. Right now, there was only the two of them. It was a dream she never wanted to end.

When at last their lips parted, he gently pulled her toward the opera house entrance and removed two tickets from his inside coat pocket. For a moment, Bianca felt like she was on a date with a movie star or a celebrity, not an alien ambassador. Soren smiled at the ticket attendant, who glanced at their tickets and waved them toward a private entrance.

"Enjoy your evening, sir." The man nodded at them as they got into an elevator that took them up one floor. They exited to find a row of gilded doors leading to private boxes.

"Wow." Bianca had been to plenty of expensive galas and other events in her life, but this felt different.

Soren opened the door to their box, and they stepped inside. The plush, gilded opera box had two comfortable-looking red velvet chairs, which were angled toward the stage on their left. People were beginning to file into the seats in the auditorium below, as well as the other boxes. Soren guided her to her seat and then went to a drink cart and pulled a champagne bottle out of a tub of ice that was waiting for them. He popped it open and poured a glass for each of them. Bianca took hers with a grin.

"I'm not one for alcohol, but I do love champagne."

Soren's eyes gleamed. "That's good to know." He took a slow sip, watching her over the rim of his glass. As far as she knew, alcohol didn't affect Krinar the way it did humans, but he was drinking to make her feel comfortable. He looked so damn sexy in his dark-gray formal three-piece suit. It had to have been custom tailored, with the way it perfectly accented his muscled form. He leaned back against the edge of the box, watching her.

"Alcohol doesn't affect you guys that much, right?" She nodded at the glass in his hands, wondering if he would tell her the truth.

"Correct."

"Can I... Can I ask more about you? The Krinar, I mean?" She scooched forward in her chair.

"I will tell you all that I am allowed."

"Okay, so about the blood. Why do you drink it?"

His lips twitched, and he took another drink before he answered. "There was once a primate species called the lonar on our planet. We hunted them and drank their blood because it gave us a much-needed hemoglobin that we were lacking. But a plague struck the lonar, and they began to die out. By then we were working together as a race to survive. It was around the time the lonar became extinct that we created synthetic blood to drink."

Bianca digested this carefully. "Okay... So why does it feel good when you bite me? Surely I'm not just having a kinky reaction to my teenage vampire fantasies."

Soren let out a deep, rich laugh that warmed her insides.

"Our saliva, when introduced into your bloodstream, has a..." He struggled for a word. "*Calming* effect on humans. We developed this trait to make our prey more manageable while we fed on the lonar. With humans, it seems to have a more sexual effect on you, and for us, perhaps because we're much closer species. Of course, you're less close to us in DNA than, say, gorillas. The lonar were a food source, not a potential mating species. You humans, however, are much closer to us—and could in the future suit such a purpose." He paused, their eyes meeting as those words sank in, and she couldn't help but picture having a child with Soren. Would it have her eyes or his? Her lighter hair or his darker hair? Would it be tall and strong or favor more human characteristics? The biologist side of her was undeniably fascinated, and the human female part of her blushed with the thought.

"It's important that we not feed from humans too often, or else a human could be drained. So we now have our clubs offer saliva injections rather than actual bites. That way humans can experience the freeing sexual highs without any of the drawbacks of losing blood."

"But you bit me. Twice," Bianca reminded him.

"I did." He chuckled and walked over to sit in the chair beside her. "Because you are my charl, I may drink from you whenever I wish, and given that you tempt me at every moment, it will be a duty of mine to resist the call of your blood. But the bites I took were small and quick. It was more to get a taste of you, not to drink." He brushed the hair back from her neck, and his gaze lingered on the vulnerable skin of her throat. Bianca felt like a Victorian heroine facing Count Dracula, but she had to admit, it made her hot just thinking about his teeth sinking into her neck while he pounded inside her until she couldn't remember her name.

The lights above them flashed, indicating the ballet was about to begin. Soren refilled her champagne glass, and then they settled back as the orchestra began to play the opening musical suite. Bianca's eyes widened as she recognized the hauntingly familiar strains.

"Tchaikovsky's *Sleeping Beauty*?" she whispered. Soren nodded. "Oh God, I've always wanted to see this ballet."

"I know."

She reached for his hand automatically, needing to

hold some part of him, to feel a deeper connection as the red velvet curtains rose and the ballet began.

She held her breath throughout the first act, watching the doomed princess dance among her suitors until the black fairy, cloaked in a dark robe, slipped into the grand ball and presented her with a bouquet of roses. Within those roses, the deadly spindle was hidden. Bianca listened to the eerie strains of music, knowing the spell of the spindle would be far too great for the heroine to resist.

The dancer spun, and her colorful gown swirled as she pirouetted and balanced on her pointed shoes until she pricked her finger on the spindle. Princess Aurora crumpled gracefully and tragically to the ground. The dark fairy prowled closer, swirling her cloak over the princess's prone form, hiding her from the view of the three beloved fairies who wanted to rescue her.

Bianca was so lost in the moment that she tensed when she realized Soren had lifted her from her own chair and settled her onto his lap. He kissed the sensitive skin just behind her ear. She tried to look his way, but he guided her face back to the stage.

"Watch them and let me play with you," he murmured in that dark, seductive voice that sent spirals of excitement and anticipation through her.

It was next to impossible now to focus on the ballet, as Soren did indeed play with her. His hands roamed her body, cupping each breast and pinching her aroused nipples. He gripped her throat, not to squeeze, but merely to hold her against him as he slid a hand between her thighs and parted her panties with a finger before delving inside to stroke the folds of her sex.

Dark pleasure began to build inside her as she realized he was going to finger her right there on the balcony during the middle of the ballet. Her eyes flashed around the opera house, trying to see if anyone was watching them. But they were more or less isolated in their box, and all eyes were on the stage. The prince was dancing through the woods now, and he stopped to stare at the vision of the cursed princess asleep in the tower as the three good fairies revealed it to him.

"That is how I feel when I see you," Soren whispered. "That you are a vision of loveliness, a goddess, one I would wait forever to possess, to make *my own*." His fingers slid inside her, and she covered her own mouth to silence the moan that would have otherwise escaped her. He stroked, coaxed, and teased her until he found that small ridge deep inside her and rubbed against it. Her legs turned to jelly, and she was grateful she wasn't standing—otherwise, she would have melted into a puddle at his feet.

Bianca gripped the armrests of the chair, squirming as he continued to play with her, teasing and stroking her like a master harpist. When he bit down on her bare shoulder, she jolted as a climax hit her in full force. She almost bit her tongue to keep from screaming as she tensed, her channel clenching desperately around his finger.

Her vision blurred, the dancers on the stage ahead of her spinning in circles almost as fast as those in her mind as she slumped back against Soren. He growled in approval and kissed her cheek.

When her eyes blinked open after several long moments, she found herself on the floor of the box. His body was on top of hers, her dress shoved up to her hips. She welcomed him, gasping in hungry delight as he thrust into her, taking her in the way she needed. That one tiny bite was as drugging and deliciously dangerous as the prick of a finger on an enchanted spindle.

The sounds of Tchaikovsky's ballet drowned her in dark, sweet dreams as Soren made love to her. She imagined herself lying prone on the bed, cobwebs clinging to the faded royal fabrics of the bedspread, a spindle lying on the floor beside her. Soren knelt at her side and leaned in, his lips covering hers as he gave her a kiss to wake her from the cursed sleep. Reality and dreams blurred together as she drowned in the sweetness of Soren's touch until she knew no more.

———

SOREN CARRIED HIS SLEEPING CHARL FROM THE PRIVATE ballet box. He'd taken care to fix her clothes, and he'd fabricated a light coat for her so she wouldn't be chilled in the foggy London night. As he carried her out of the elevator, the attendant met them.

"Is she all right?"

Soren nodded. "She enjoyed the show, but I fear the jet lag has caught up with her."

The attendant nodded. "Poor thing. Jet lag can be difficult. Have a good day, sir."

"And you." He exited the opera house, glad the crowds had thinned. He didn't want to have to fight his way through a group of people while carrying Bianca in his arms. He spotted a row of black cabs along the curb and deposited Bianca in the back seat before he climbed in beside her.

"Where to?"

"The Ritz." He had booked a suite for them tonight because he wanted to enjoy the evening with her. While she was still on American time, it was late at night in London, and the city would be asleep in a few hours. Soren planned to spend those hours with his charl in a bed.

By the time the cab pulled up to the hotel, Bianca had woken up and was able to walk with him, although she yawned the whole way to the door. A doorman decked out in a fine uniform greeted them.

Bianca's eyes widened as she took in the size and lavish quality of the Ritz's lobby.

Soren checked in at the front desk, and then they took an elevator to the Prince of Wales Suite. Bright and bold fabrics on the chairs and couches were luxuriously arranged alongside the delicate gold filigree rosewood furniture and a fire had been lit in the fireplace. Service at the Ritz was rumored to be the best. He grinned as he saw the bottle of wine and two glasses set out on the table between the two couches near the fireplace. That would be excellent for later.

Soren carried his little prize to the bath and stripped her of her clothes. He poured in a small bottle of bubble bath he found on the side of the overlarge tub as he ran the hot water. Bianca sighed in delight as she slipped inside. She rubbed her legs together and splashed around a bit before she leaned her head back on the tub and closed her eyes. Soren sat on the edge of the tub, gazing down at her—his beautiful, alluring charl.

"You make me crazy, you know that?" she said with a sigh, and it startled him. He thought she was asleep by now.

"I can't tell if that's an insult or a compliment." He stroked the top of her head, loving the feel of her hair, soft and silky beneath his fingers.

"Mostly a compliment," she murmured, leaning into his touch. "I had my life together. I had my plans.

And then you just came in and made me throw it all out the window. I was shy before, and now I'm naked in a tub with you after we had sex in a private box in a London opera house." Her eyes opened, and she tilted her head back to look up at him.

"Before three days ago, I commanded the respect and trust of my people," Soren said. "Now I'm removed from my job, and I lost respect from my peers. I may even be facing exile from Earth, all because of how you make me feel."

She reached up and their hands met, hers wet to his dry, and he laced their fingers together.

"I'm sorry," she whispered. "I didn't know you'd lose so much just to be with me."

"It isn't your fault. It was my choice." He paused, squeezing her hand. "And I would do it again and again."

She shifted in the water and suddenly smiled.

"What?" he asked, enjoying her amusement even though he didn't know the source.

"I was thinking about sea otters. Have you ever seen one?"

"I think, perhaps once. Sea mammals. Mustelidae family. Chubby, furry, black noses, adorable, right?"

"Yes," she laughed. "They also happen to be my favorite animal. They are one of the reasons I want to work at the Monterey Bay Aquarium. They have an amazing view of an underwater kelp forest."

She closed her eyes, as if picturing it right now. Soren waited for her to continue.

"Sea otters do something no other species does. You know what it is?"

"I'm afraid I don't." Soren continued to hold her hand, marveling at the sense of peace that filled him. Touching Bianca like this, connecting his soul to hers by only their hands, was powerful enough to banish the memories that haunted him of his time as a prisoner on Zaruth.

"Sea otters hold on to each other when they sleep. Their little paws curl around each other like they're holding hands. It stops them from drifting away on the sea, but it also bonds them. Can you imagine? A species so small, not as emotionally complex as humans or dolphins, yet they experience the importance of bonding to one another, of never letting go."

He understood what she was telling him, and his hold on her hand tightened. "I will never drift away from you, little one."

"But I will grow old. What happens when I'm no longer young and beautiful like you?" She looked away, but not before he saw the bright shine of tears in her eyes.

He released her hand so he could kneel down beside the tub and turn her face to his.

"You mustn't worry about that."

She stared at him, her bottom lip quivering. "But it won't make sense for you to want me then."

"My little scientist." He sighed, smiled a little, and traced her lips with his thumb. "I shouldn't tell you anything, but you make me shatter the rules." She waited, curiosity blending with trepidation in her gaze. "As my charl, you could be injected with nanocytes. They actively repair your body, right down to your DNA, indefinitely." He paused, wondering if she would understand what he was saying.

"Nanotechnology? Like...repairing cells to maintain peak health?"

"And even reverse age damage," he added.

She stared at him, her lips slightly parted. "That's how the Krinar stay young?"

"Yes. And as my charl, the right of that technology would be extended to you."

Bianca still held his hand, but her eyes turned distant in a way that worried him. "Do you understand time, Soren?"

"Time? Yes, the measuring of minutes, hours, days, and years." He brushed her hair again, wishing he could erase the sorrow reflected in her eyes.

"You understand it as a theory, something you can calculate and measure. But humans see it differently. It's something we face in a way you can't. Time is an enemy, sure, but it's also an old friend. It makes you feel alive and blessed, and then one morning, cursed as you enter the twilight years of your life. It's a sense of being, a sense of feeling oneself in a bigger way. You'd be handing me immortality and taking away the journey of life. Everyone I love would die. My father, my friends..."

Soren couldn't bear the sorrow in his sweet, brave, beautiful charl. He scooped her up, not caring that she was soaking wet. Bianca gasped and wrapped her arms around his neck. He carried her to the bed and set her down, still holding her close as he leaned back against the headboard. Her green eyes reminded him of the deep forest outside his parents' home on Krina. It was the color of life, the color of intensity. Here on Earth, it could be the color of jealousy, and a dozen more emotions could be reflected in a dozen shades of green. To him, Bianca's green eyes were that of life unending.

"I understand time, little one, just as you described. In a way, it weighs upon me more than it could any human. I have borne witness to eight millennia of changes. I've watched empires rise and fall. I've seen great civilizations turn into rain forests and witnessed the last warriors of ancient races seclude themselves deep in the hills as the languages of their old ways faded into obscurity. I've seen devastation and creation obliterate and blossom on this planet. I have watched and waited alone, until I saw you." How could he put into words what she meant to him? How important it was for her to remain by his side, now and forever?

Soren pressed his forehead to hers, closing his eyes as he inhaled her feminine aroma with a lingering hint of lemon from the hotel soap.

"You... You are a change in my unchanging life. Do you understand?" He dared to open his eyes, afraid of what he would see, but Bianca's eyes were full of tears, and she sniffed and shifted closer to him.

"Okay," she whispered, the single word spoken with determination.

"Okay?" He had to be sure of what she was telling him. That she agreed to be his, knowing what the future held.

"Okay," she echoed. Then she kissed him, her tongue lashing against his lips, and his blood sang with desire and longing. She would someday know the gift she was to him—he would find a way to show her. But for now, he would start with this.

He rolled atop her gloriously naked body, shedding his clothes. Her eyes swept over his skin, and he marveled at the gold tan of his flesh against her creamy pale skin. She parted her legs and was still biting her lip shyly as he gently entered her. This joining between them was not one born of the madness to mate. This was a deeper connection that showed what lay between them went beyond physical desire.

Soren worshiped Bianca's body with kisses and caresses. He stroked her tender folds and the sensitive nub of her clit, nibbling her earlobes and the curves of her hips. Then he entered her again, teasing her with slow, deep thrusts. She called out his name over and over, her nails digging into his back as they came hard, their shared climax bursting with a swell of passion. She shivered beneath him, and he could feel her flutter around his shaft. He groaned softly, burying his face against her neck.

At that moment, he was utterly captivated by her heart, her mind, and her body. He pressed little kisses to her face, wanting to cover every inch of her, and she let him. Her hands roved over his muscles, stroking, kneading, exploring, though with no sense of urgency.

As their uneven breathing slowed to a calm, measured pace, he rolled off her and pulled her back to spoon against him. His cock twitched and she wriggled her bottom, but he knew she didn't mean to tease him. She drifted to sleep soon after, and Soren lay there, holding her in his arms, lost in his own thoughts.

He didn't want to steal her from her life here or her friends or family, nor did he wish to hide from the world forever, leading double lives. But she was his. There was no going back now. There had to be a way to convince her father, Arus, and the Council to accept them as they were.

He trailed his fingers along her skin, watching her sleep and thanking the universe for finding her. The trick now was how to keep her.

10

"You've got it bad for him, girl," Claudia said as she watched Bianca prepare for another night out with Soren.

"I do," Bianca admitted. She chose a pair of gold earrings that were in the shape of leaves and slipped them on.

She brushed her hair back and watched the dangling gold leaves dance. Finals were almost over, and the last few weeks had been an amazing whirlwind of studying followed by passionate outings with Soren where he enchanted her mind and heart with some amazing activity, and then he'd seduce her body in bed. She'd stopped caring long ago that she'd become his personal sex toy. She knew what she meant to him now, that what was growing between them was so much more than she ever could have dreamed with any other man, let alone an alien.

"So what's the plan tonight?" Claudia had been keeping a running list of Bianca's nights out and had been more or less living vicariously through her.

"I think we're going to the aquarium in Monterey Bay."

"Your favorite place? He's one smart alien." Claudia watched her pull on a navy-blue sundress. "You don't usually wear dresses. What's that about?"

Bianca flushed, too embarrassed to admit Claudia was right. She didn't really like dresses, but they had one huge positive. They gave Soren easier access to her. She had quickly come to like how he pinned her up against a wall and ripped her panties off and fucked her until she screamed out his name. He was a god in bed and out, and part of her wanted the world to know it.

"I'm going to assume by the color of your face it's because of something to do with Soren and accessibility?" Claudia raised her eyebrows, and Bianca stifled a laugh as she nodded.

"Boy, you guys didn't waste any time on that front, huh?"

Claudia collected a set of highlighters scattered like rainbow lollipops on her bed and set them in a pencil cup on her nightstand.

"There really isn't a slow speed for these guys. They

just kiss you and you're done for." It was true. Having a Krinar lover made a person forget things like rationality. It was all wild lust, raw sex, and mind-blowing pleasure with them. And in Soren's case, it was all wrapped up in an expensive, adventurous package.

Since their secret rendezvous had begun, they had gone to a ballet, a gala celebrating a new masters painting exhibit in Paris, and a cherry blossom festival in China. He was showing her the beauty of Earth and the beauty of humanity. She'd been convinced for years that the Krinar viewed humans as an inferior race, unable to take care of themselves or their planet. But now she was starting to see a difference. Soren didn't see her as infantile. He saw her as an equal.

"You're being careful, right?" Claudia asked.

"Careful?"

"Yeah, you know, condoms, birth control..."

"Um, well, here's the thing—according to Soren, Krinar and humans can't get pregnant together. And we don't share any diseases. The Krinar can't catch them from us, and they don't have any of their own to give us." She had known that even before she started sleeping with Soren.

As the president's daughter, she had heard a lot of things, including scientific briefings from the US government branch that was partnered with the Krinar. The Krinar gave the United States and other countries limited but useful information about their biology—like the fact that Krinar couldn't get or spread STDs—but nothing that could possibly be used against them. Knowing that, the panic level had been drastically reduced once the fear of an alien plague was off the table.

"Seriously?" Claudia's eyes widened. "We don't need to use protection? Score!" She punched the air in a goofy way.

Bianca laughed. "It's not something you can share, okay? That's private info, protected by the government."

Claudia mimed zipping her lips. "Mum's the word."

"Thanks." Bianca retrieved a pair of navy-blue wedges with cork bottoms to match her dress and slipped them on. Finally, she grabbed a thin white cardigan button-up sweater to complete the look.

"Be back by midnight, young lady," Claudia warned in a mother hen voice. They both burst out laughing.

"Yes, Mom," she giggled. She pressed the groove in her cuff and vanished from sight. She left the dorm, waved to the poor agents—who still hadn't caught on—with a giggle, and ran to meet Soren's ship. He was waiting for her, and he caught her in his arms, kissing her hard. Then they both climbed into his ship and headed for the West Coast.

Once at the Monterey Bay Aquarium, she saw that the parking lot was empty.

"Soren, it looks like it's closed." She couldn't deny

the sting of disappointment. "I should have checked the hours before we left."

Soren chuckled. "It's closed, but not for us. Come." He gestured for her to turn off her stealth cuff, and he did the same. He grasped her hand in his, and they walked up to the entrance. An aquarium employee greeted them.

"Ambassador Soren, we are honored by your visit. We're also pleased to welcome your anonymous guest." The young woman in the polo shirt and khaki shorts winked at Bianca before she motioned for them to follow her. She led them through an eerily quiet maze of exhibits. It was beautiful. Fish swam in tanks on either side and then overhead as they walked through an underwater glass tunnel. Bianca gasped as they reached the kelp forest room. A table with a crisp white linen cloth had been set for two, candles were already lit, and a vase of wildflowers sat in the center, filling the room with a floral scent.

"We will have dinner served soon, but please help yourself to the champagne." The aquarium employee waved toward a drink cart that had been set up by the table.

"Thank you, Candace," Soren said. The woman nodded and then left them alone.

Bianca stared at Soren, then at the table.

"How on earth did you arrange all this?" she asked, her heart racing as he stepped closer, curling one arm around her waist. Their bodies fit so perfectly together, even though he was a foot taller than her.

"I might have provided extra funding for several species reintroduction programs and coastline preservation campaigns."

"Really?" Her heart swelled as she gazed up at him.

"Of course. This planet is beautiful. I want to protect it. But I also know how much it means to you. Lucky for me, your interests and mine are one and the same."

"So logical—how like a K," she teased, poking him in the chest with a finger.

"Logical? I suppose I haven't done a good enough job reminding you how much of an animal I can be." His eyes heated as he let his gaze rove over her body, but he didn't move to kiss her. Instead, he released her waist and nodded toward the kelp forest windows.

Then her eyes moved to the tall twenty-foot-high windows. The setting sun illuminated the water's surface, which turned the tops of the tall kelp stalks a reddish gold. The coloring tapered back into a deep rich green down toward the roots at the base of the aquarium. She moved closer and pressed her hands to the thick glass, her eyes devouring the beautiful sight. The kelp swayed slightly as the water moved in a rhythm designed to mimic the ocean waves.

A large school of fish billowed out near her against the glass before banking sharply to the right. The silver flash they gave off was almost blinding in its beauty. Small nurse sharks, babies no longer than her arm, swam lazily around the winding tendrils of the kelp. Far above, Bianca could make out the otters, floating above her on the surface. Occasionally, one would dive below and swirl through the kelp, chasing small fish before heading back up to the surface.

Soren stood behind her, one arm wound tenderly around her waist again.

"You sure know how to woo a girl." She laughed, but her heart suddenly sank into doubt. Had he done this with other women? Not here or even on this planet, of course, but out there over the span of centuries. He'd certainly had the time.

"I've not had much practice until you," he admitted.

Bianca wasn't sure she could believe him. He was too gorgeous, too sweet, too available for too long. How had the women of Krina not been fighting over him?

"In all those years, there had to have been many women. I mean, the Krinar don't exactly have the sexual hang-ups humans have."

His hand around her waist rubbed her belly. "Of course. There have been a few over the years, but they have been encounters meant only to satisfy lust." He set their champagne flutes down and turned her in his arms.

She had a moment to admire him in the undulating glow of the lights from the tall windows. There was no hint of deception lurking there, no hint of superiority or any other negative emotion. She saw only passion and tenderness.

"I wish you could see things the way I do, how long I've lived, so that you can understand me when I say you are it for me, Bianca. There will be no other after you. We will be together *always*." He slowly closed the distance between them, and his lips touched hers. He played with her tongue, soft but erotic, showing her that wicked gift he offered as a lover.

Her heart throbbed in excitement as she met his kisses, her arms twining around his neck. It was a pure and sensual experience, kissing Soren in the rich green glowing light of the kelp forest viewing room. The world around them was bathed in soft emerald and deep blue, and the sound of water rocking against the glass calmed her as much as his mouth excited her.

They would make love in this room soon, she knew, and it would feel as though they were in a dream within a dream. Her body quickened in the way it always did with the promise of the word *soon*. How silly she'd been to fear this man. *Soon* was not a word to fear, but to embrace. Soren pulled her deeper into him, but a moment later they broke apart as a man brought in a tray of food.

"I'm so sorry," the man whispered, his face beet red. He set out two salads and a pair of vegetarian dishes on the table, then quickly made his exit. Bianca covered her face, shoulders shaking in silent laughter.

"Why don't we eat?"

Bianca agreed, and Soren pulled her chair out for her. She accepted the chivalrous gesture and raised her champagne glass toward him.

"A toast," she proposed. He responded by raising his own glass. "To peaceful relations between our peoples."

He touched the rim of his glass to hers, and with a mischievous twinkle in his eyes, he added, "And to passionate relations as well."

She was still smiling as she sipped her champagne. The bubbles made her want to giggle. He knew just how to get her relaxed but keep her on the edge of her seat at the same time.

They ate their meal and talked for almost an hour, enjoying the quiet solitude without fear of being seen by anyone who would report them to the Krinar or to her father.

"Tell me something about you, Soren. Something secret," she asked, wanting to play a game to learn more about him. In many ways, he'd lived quite a life, and she wanted to know more about him.

"Something secret?" he mused, his fingertips playing with the stem of his champagne flute.

"Yes. I mean, we're going to be spending a lot of

time together, aren't we? I should probably know everything there is to know about you."

His gaze turned distant as he thought it over. "I was young and foolish once, determined to prove my worth. I traveled to a distant planet called Zaruth in hopes of making contact with a new species and a potential home for my people. I was captured during my exploration of their world."

She gasped. "Captured?" She'd expected him to share some amusing anecdote, not something so serious.

"The people of this planet, the Kronosians, were twice my size and twice as strong. I was curious to see if it was close enough to Krina to be seeded by our people for a future home world. But I didn't account for the native people. What Kronosians lacked in technology they made up for in brute strength. I was not able to stop them. They had developed a natural drug from a plant native to their planet. They laced their weapons with it, and when I tried to fight them off to get back to my ship, I was wounded. The drug rendered me as weak as a child, and the nanocytes couldn't repair me quickly enough to defend myself. I was too far from my ship and couldn't stop them when they grabbed and bound me."

The darkness in his eyes pulled her to him in a way she'd never expected. Her heart pounded as she imagined him, a young handsome Krinar, fighting off a horde of Kronosians and losing.

"My ship was cloaked, so I knew they would not find it, but as for me..." A tic worked in his jaw. "I was not so lucky. They were puzzled and afraid of my arrival, taking it as some ill omen. The translating device installed behind my ear took weeks to adapt and learn their tongue. By the time I was able to communicate in their tongue, they had decided I was a danger to them. They cast me into what they called the Wailing Pit. I landed on the bones of their condemned brothers, ones who'd perished by starvation. They expected me to die after a few days without food or water."

Bianca reached across the table, clasping his hand tightly.

"But you didn't."

He shook his head.

"Because of the nanocytes?"

"Correct. There were two other prisoners there when I was first pushed into the pit. I knew they would die slowly and painfully from starvation. I gave them a quick death, drinking their blood until they passed. Their hemoglobin was just enough to survive on, but I became a shell, a creature driven only by instincts. Each time they cast someone down into the pit, I did what I had to do to survive. I killed hundreds of them —males, females, even some younger Kronosians.

Whoever landed beside me, bleeding and injured, I granted them death and took the blood I needed to survive. After three centuries, the Kronosians forgot I was down there. Eventually, the bones of their people rose so high that I had a chance to climb out. I made it to freedom and dragged my weakened body to my ship and returned home."

"You were in that pit for *three hundred years*?" Bianca's eyes widened. She could not imagine that horror. The isolation he must have felt, the crushing loss of hope...and having to kill over and over just to survive.

"Everyone on Krina believed I was dead. Only Sef believed I was still alive."

Bianca frowned at Sef's name. Soren didn't miss it.

"My twin and I were close. Despite the fight you witnessed, I trust him with my life. I would trust him with yours as well."

"But he hurt you..."

"He got the better of me that time." He smiled then and left her confused. "I knew I had wronged you, taking you away like that. Sef reminded me of that, and I deserved a lesson in humility. Someday, when it's safe for us to be together in the open, I would like you to meet him again. You will like him. I promise you." He turned her hand over beneath his, clasping her palm in his.

"I'm so sorry that happened to you, Soren. I can't even imagine..."

He urged her to stand, and she came around the table so he could pull her into his lap. He buried his face in her neck, pressing kisses to her skin to soothe her when she wanted to soothe him.

"It was a long time ago. Long enough to heal," he whispered in her ear, then nibbled on her earlobe. "Now, tell me something secret about you."

She fought off a moan. The attention he was giving her made it hard to think at all. She wondered what she could tell him that even mattered compared to his story.

"I want to make a difference," she said. "To help not only people, but the planet. It's why I want to be a marine biologist. Our lives depend on the oceans, and most of us don't even realize it. I want to help and protect the creatures that live there. If we lose the balance there, we're all doomed."

She looked toward the kelp forest, and her heart beat fast with joy. "I look at the world, the colors, the creatures great and small, all living in an ancient circle of life and death and rebirth, and I feel there's something greater out there? Something glorious that pulls all the pieces of this magnificent puzzle together. I used to think that made me feel small, but now I feel... endless. As if I'm part of all that. Each time I step into the shallows to help an injured seal or run a blood test on a sick pelican, I'm a positive part of the circle." She laughed. "I'm not making sense, am I?"

He caught her chin and turned her head to face him. Their eyes locked, green to golden brown.

"You hold the universe inside you, and all the majesty that comes with it. I understand. Even as I lay suffering in my prison so far from home, I would marvel whenever it would rain upon my skin, feeling the infinite power of life in each drop. It was a small hope, but hope nonetheless, to stay alive and get home. That hope, infinitesimal as it was most days, was a constant source of wonder to me. How could I live another day if I were not *destined* to survive? Long after I came home, I continued to search for that destiny, that reason I stayed alive. Then, when I saw you again outside the Princeton president's office, frightened as you were of me, I saw that same determination in your eyes to survive. That was when you became my universe, my endless wonder."

He touched his nose to hers, nuzzling her, his breath mingling with her own. It was like lying outside on a perfect spring day, cool velvet grass beneath her and endless blue sky above her on a day that would last forever.

She closed her eyes as she leaned deeper into him. "How do you do that?"

"Do what?" he asked between kisses that made her blood sing and her heart throb in a wild rhythm.

"Make me crazy for you, like you're the only thing I could ever need."

He laughed softly, the sweet sound of his delight turning her on. "Because we are meant to be, *lilana*. You are my charl, and I'm your cheren. Our bodies recognize each other's unique and perfect chemistry. It's a rare thing to feel devoted to another on all levels, not simply physical. We are special, Bianca. It's why I defied my people to be with you."

He stroked her bottom lip with his thumb, and she couldn't resist nipping him. Soren's eyes melted into a bright tawny gold as he watched her suck his finger into her mouth. She felt him go hard beneath her thighs, and she wriggled her bottom to tease him.

"Don't do that," he warned in a deep growl that might have scared her in another life.

She let his finger escape her lips in a soft pop. "Do what?"

"You know full well." His eyes held a predatory gleam as he slid her off his lap and pushed her to her knees. He grasped her hair in one hand. "Perhaps I should make you take the edge off my hunger." He nodded at the bulge in his pants.

Bianca was eager to take him like this, to hold a measure of power over him—dominating her K lover by controlling his pleasure. She licked her lips and reached for his pants, undoing them. His thick cock stood there erect, and her body flushed as she looked back up at him. She saw the wild look in his eyes.

"If you take me in your mouth, I can't promise to be gentle."

"Maybe I don't want gentle." She curled her fingers around his shaft, squeezing it. He hissed out a breath. She lowered her head and licked the tip of him, relishing the salty taste of his skin before she took him inside her mouth. He couldn't fit all the way, so she closed one hand around the rest of him while she sucked and licked and pulled. The hand in her hair tightened as he began to lift his hips in her direction. She moved closer to him at the same time.

He groaned and pushed her head down on him a little harder, making her take more of him, but the feeling of him losing so much control that he was this desperate to fuck her mouth was impossible not to enjoy.

She took it all, loving the way he spun out of control. Just before she expected him to come, he pulled her up and turned her around. He swept a hand across the table, smashing dishes and extinguishing candles as the vase of flowers splashed water everywhere. He bent her over the table and shoved her dress up over her hips. He tugged her panties down to her knees and rammed himself deep inside her. The angle of penetration was new, and she groaned at being so suddenly and unexpectedly stretched and filled, but she was so wet and it felt so good for him to be inside her that it didn't matter.

He fucked her raw, gripping her hips hard enough to leave bruises, but she didn't give a damn. She'd just heal up later. It felt amazing to be owned by her dark Krinar lover, to feel him use her, giving her pleasure in return, all the while knowing how much he cared for her, how precious she was to him. A woman could get high on such thoughts alone, but Soren offered so much more. Sweet, intoxicating passion pounded through her heart, chest, and head in exquisite harmony with Soren's body. As the release hit, all she saw was a blinding, glorious galaxy of stars shattering into bursts of color against the backs of her eyelids.

Waves of ecstasy rolled through her as the orgasm continued for a full minute. When he finally joined her in climax, she felt his release heat her insides. He expelled a panting rhythm of breaths against the back of her neck. He murmured soft words in his native tongue, creating a deep lullaby of sensuality as he brushed gentle fingertips through her hair and over her ears and neck.

"So sweet, so tight and hot, my little Bianca," he purred before he withdrew from her.

Her inner walls twitched over and over, leaving her stinging and aching for him to fill her again. He chuckled as he ran a finger between her wet folds and then inserted it into her. She whimpered, desperate for another release, yet never wanting him to stop this tender torture. He cupped her ass with his other hand

and gave it a playful smack. She yelped, then sighed as he soothed the spot, still slowly penetrating her with his finger, soon drawing a second climax from her. It was softer than the first, but it made her knees weak. She gripped the edges of the table, writhing in pleasure until at last it faded.

"Oh God" was all she could say in a breathless pant as he wiped her clean and pulled her panties back up. Then he sat back down and pulled her across his lap once more, cradling her as she burrowed into him. They had broken through some barrier, some limitation she hadn't even realized existed until tonight. It had pushed her beyond her comfort zone, and she liked it. Perhaps a little too much.

"Bianca," he murmured. "*Malenkai sovenyah*."

"What's that mean?" she mumbled against his chest.

His laugh warmed her clear down to her toes. "It means 'my endless wonder.'"

"How are you so perfect?" Bianca asked as he carried her through the darkened aquarium.

"Because I was made for you," he answered. "The universe has destined us for each other."

She had no doubt that he was right.

She was only half-awake when he carried her to his ship. She blinked, slowly watching the setting sun disappear beneath the horizon. Soren pressed something on the ship's console, and everything around them vanished. This was new. The ship wasn't just cloaked on the outside but on the inside as well! They were flying through the air with nothing blocking their view of the ground below. Bianca gasped.

"It's rather pretty to fly like this—if you aren't afraid of heights," Soren said.

Bianca's stomach fluttered, but she reached out, feeling the ship's seat still holding her securely in place, even though it looked like she was flying over clouds. She finally convinced herself to relax. Her eyes started to close again, and before she knew it, she was dreaming of them flying away from Earth and into the stars.

When she finally opened her eyes, she was being tucked into her dorm bed by her handsome Krinar lover. He had already put her in her PJs and pulled the blankets up to her chin. He saw her open her eyes and trailed a fingertip down the length of her nose and over her lips. She reached up, catching his hand, holding it close.

"Stay," she whispered in the quiet, dark room.

"I wish I could. But in time we won't be separated like this, I promise. Sleep now." He brushed his lips over hers, and she fell asleep, still tasting his kiss and dreaming of the wonders she would see in the galaxy by his side.

———

SOREN ENTERED HIS HOME IN DC AND SCOWLED. SEF was there, seated on his couch, watching his TV. His twin was watching a show called *The Bachelor* and laughing darkly.

"Can you believe this? Look at these women. Fake, idiotic fools. Who can't see through their vapid nature? Where are the genuine girls with curves and brains?" He picked up the remote to hit mute.

"Sef, aren't you supposed to be on assignment?" Soren acted calm, but he feared Sef could sense his deception through their twin connection.

"Not yet. I leave for Kansas in a month or so."

"Ah, so you're going to bunk with me in the meantime." Soren headed into the kitchen to get some juice. Sef followed him.

"You don't want me spending time with you?" Sef said, half teasing. "I can always return to the Krinar Embassy in DC and stay there."

Soren faced him. "If you wish to stay here, you know you're more than welcome." He meant it, and he knew Sef could feel it through their link.

"You've had quite a night for someone who hasn't been reassigned a new political post yet," Sef observed. He leaned back against the counter opposite his brother, crossing his arms over his chest.

Soren almost laughed at his brother, who was dressed all in black. Black shirt with some human band logo, black jeans, and biker boots. Black was a very violent color among the Krinar, yet both he and Sef found it appropriate to wear that color while on Earth. Part of him had never cared for the soft, pale colors that were commonplace in Krinar cities. It was one more thing that had made him suited to his position as ambassador. He understood Earth culture, had spent years studying it, and had found there was much to like.

"I've been going out, trying to get Bianca out of my system, as they say." Not that he ever could, but there was an element of truth to his statement that allowed him to say it with conviction. He used his hand to summon the controls in his home, and the wall opened up, providing him a fresh glass of juice. He retrieved the glass, and the wall sealed tight.

"Hmmm...that must be hard to do, given that you keep seeing her every night."

Soren stopped and lowered his glass.

"You smell of her, brother. And sex. You forgot to bathe tonight."

Soren cursed. Sef was right. He had gotten lazy tonight. But then, he hadn't expected company.

"Are you going to tell Arus?" It wasn't really a question.

Sef shrugged. "I follow orders. I had my initial orders to separate you. He hasn't told me to *keep* you separated, nor did he order me to keep tabs on your movements."

"But I thought you agreed it was a risk to peaceful relations?"

A dark humor lit his brother's eyes. "Like you, brother, I feel we should take any humans we want, especially if they want us. No one, not even the president or the Council, should stand in our way. Bianca wants you, so by rights you should be able to take her as a charl. She *does* want you, doesn't she?"

Soren sighed. "She does. We belong together, but I do not know how to claim her without causing a diplomatic crisis with President Wells."

"And the Council," Sef added, laughing. "You've got major problems, brother."

"You could stop laughing at me and actually help," Soren reminded him.

Sef stroked his chin thoughtfully. "Give me some time to think it over. Oh, you'd better call Mother and tell her you've taken a charl. You know she would love it—Father will too."

Soren snorted. "You only want me to distract them because Mother still pesters you to retire from your guardian duties."

"Perhaps," Sef muttered. "We aren't a hundred years old—you'd think she would let us live our lives and not mother us."

"I hate to remind you, Sef, but mothering is what she loves to do. Now leave me so I can shower."

Sef headed for the door but paused. "I did have a

message for you from Arus, however. He wants you to attend a state dinner tomorrow evening with President Wells. You will have to cancel your plans with Bianca, whatever they may be."

"A state dinner?" Soren was shocked.

Sef nodded. "I think Arus is trying to find a way to get you and the president to speak diplomatically again. I believe he wants to help you find a way to keep Bianca. He's a good friend."

"He is indeed." A prickling of guilt underneath Soren's skin made him frown. He owed Arus much more than he imagined, and yet here he was sneaking behind his back with Bianca, defying the Council and threatening their peace with Earth.

Soren stayed in the kitchen, thinking about what he could do. Perhaps he would have an opportunity to speak with President Wells privately. There had to be a way to convince him that Soren would take good care of Bianca. Because if he couldn't, it might cause an intergalactic war that could annihilate the humans in the blink of an eye and destroy all the Krinar plans for peaceful coexistence.

11

Bianca finished her last final, grinning as she passed her professor a completed test booklet, and then she practically skipped out of the class. There was nothing more freeing than knowing she had no more tests to take. Her cell phone vibrated, and she paused outside the building to check it. It was Soren. Mike and Scott trailed behind her, but they were far enough away that she was able to read the message without them seeing.

Soren: *Have to cancel tonight. Attending state dinner in DC. Plan to talk to your father.*

She texted back as she resumed walking.

Bianca: *Good luck with Dad. Finals went well. Miss you.*

His reply came back a second later.

Soren: *Of course they did. You are brilliant. I expected nothing less.*

She grinned. That was why she loved him. She halted in the middle of the sidewalk. Bianca absorbed the surprise of that revelation. *I love Soren. Truly love him.*

"Ms. Wells?" Mike asked, putting a hand on her shoulder.

She shoved the phone into her purse and smiled back at him.

"I'm okay." For the first time in ages, she felt that restless need she had to prove her worth to the world diminish. Being in love made her feel stronger, more determined than ever to do what she dreamed to do, yet she didn't feel as stressed as she used to about it. She almost texted him, but declarations of love were something to be done face-to-face.

She headed back to the dormitories as dusk lengthened the shadows of the old trees across the lawn. The world felt different tonight, probably because she'd realized she was in love, *real* love for the first time in her life.

Bianca waved good night to Mike and Scott and headed into her dorm. When she opened the door to her room and flicked on the lights, she gasped. Claudia lay on the floor, blood trickling from her mouth. She wasn't moving ,but she was still breathing.

"Claudia!" She rushed toward her friend, but

before she could reach her, someone grabbed her from behind. She tried to scream, but a hand covered her mouth and a cloth smothered her nose. She was too panicked not to inhale the sickly-sweet scent. Her vision blurred at the edges like a watercolor painting as she tried to hold her breath. She tried to reach for the panic button on her wrist, but it was covered by her assailant's other hand. Bianca went limp and tried not to breathe, hoping to fool him into thinking she was already unconscious. But he held on to her still, waiting, until she couldn't hold her breath any longer. The world dwindled into terrifying darkness as she at last inhaled.

When she came to, she was on a cold concrete floor. Her hands were bound with rope, too tight for her to move. She tried but couldn't reach the groove on her stealth cuff. A pulsing pain beat behind her eyes, and her stomach cramped with nausea. She'd been dosed with chloroform. Mike and Scott had trained her to recognize the different effects of drugs that might be used on her if she were ever abducted. She curled in on herself, unable to stop a moan from escaping. The dark concrete walls reverberated with the noise, the echoing sound mocking her.

"Looks like she's awake. Make the call," a woman said. The muffled sound came from behind the solitary door.

Bianca lifted her head and squinted through the

gloom. The large metal door had a sliding peephole. A man's face was partially visible, watching her.

She knew better than to engage with this man. It wouldn't do her any good until she had a sense of the reason she was being held and who her captors might be. The latch slid closed, hiding her from view, and she struggled to sit up. The nest of old rags and threadbare blankets beneath her smelled of vomit and mildew.

Bianca gagged as she brushed the blankets away. She studied the cell, looking for weak spots the way she'd been trained. Water dripped down part of one wall, pooling in a corner. The *drip–drip–drip* was a steady beat inside her head, making her headache that much worse. A tiny window too high up for her to reach allowed light to pierce the gloom, but the window glass was stained with years of grime. She closed her eyes. She could hear the faint sound of wind through the metal door and saw the light dancing under its edge as two people stood just outside.

"Mr. President, I assume you're standing next to Ambassador Soren. If you want your daughter to live, you'll put him on the phone. *Now*."

There was a moment of silence, and then the man spoke again.

"This is the Anti-K Resistance, Ambassador Soren. We have your human pet. If you want her, she'll be at this address—271 Meadow Lawn Drive, the old tire factory in Princeton." There was silence, and then

"What do you *think* we want? For you Ks to leave our planet and never return."

Bianca listened harder. Whatever Soren said made the man furious. "I will kill her." The metal door swung open, and a man in a ski mask entered. He pointed a gun straight at her head. "Beg me for your life, traitor," he demanded. Bianca stared at the gun and looked back up to him.

"Go to hell!" The words came out fainter than she wanted because her head was still foggy. She scrambled to her feet and tried to back away, but she hit the corner.

"You first, K-loving bitch."

Bang!

Pain exploded in her leg, and she screamed. The man put his gun away and turned the cell phone camera at her. She reached for her shin, crying out as she stared at the wound in her leg.

"You see that? Get your alien ass here and you can have her, but only after we see you guys getting in your ships and leaving. Try anything dumb, and you can have what's *left* of her."

The agony started to fade to something more tolerable, and she slumped onto her side, her body starting to twitch. She was in shock. The thought tumbled in her head as her blood dripped on the cement in time with the water leak next to her.

Someone laughed. The sound was cold and cruel. But it wasn't the man who'd shot her.

Glassy-eyed with pain, Bianca stared up at a woman who was looking down at her through the open doorway.

"You guys don't mess around," the woman said to the man who'd shot her.

She wasn't wearing a ski mask. Bianca tried to focus on her, memorizing details—her frizzy hair and cruel eyes framed by overlarge glasses. There was something familiar about her. It suddenly clicked.

"You...the crazy tabloid owner..." Bianca remembered her from the news. Unable to find any real dirt on her father, she'd printed fabricated stories about him, stirring up outrage and controversy, all so she could sell a few more papers.

"I'm not crazy!" The woman tried to grab the gun from the man in the ski mask. He yanked it out of her reach and shoved her hard enough that she stumbled back a step.

"Just let me shoot her!" she yelled.

"Not yet." The man tilted his head, staring down at Bianca with cold, dark eyes. "We have a plan, remember?"

"Yes, well...as long as you kill her and the K bastard when he comes for her," the woman muttered. "I don't think they will actually *leave*, but we can at least get one killed and find a way to pin the blame on them. It will be perfect. Even the K-lovers will turn on them."

"And then we have a *real* revolution." The man's smile, just visible through the ski mask opening, was cruel as he continued to gaze at Bianca in a way that made her skin crawl. "You should leave, Tarah. I'm going to set the fuses to the building. We'll monitor the scene from a safe distance. Once the K enters the building, we'll level the place."

"Good. It will make for a perfect K terrorist story. Soren's own people had them both killed to keep them apart. Everyone will be furious on both sides."

Bianca had to find a way to warn Soren. She bit back a cry of pain as she crawled toward the door that they had left partially open. She wasn't going to go down without a fight. But the second she reached the door, it slammed shut in her face, and the bolt slid into the lock.

She was trapped.

———

TEN MINUTES EARLIER…

Soren was bored. These silly political state dinners were never as entertaining as they pretended to be. Only politicians and their spouses came. Soren desperately wished the scientists, poets, dreamers, and "doers" of this world were in this room instead. Earth's best and brightest—like Bianca. Those were the people who should be meeting and talking. They would share ideas, build bridges, change the world. Not this back-patting nonsense.

He glanced toward President Wells, who looked just as bored as he was. That wasn't shocking. Wells was a "doer," and he didn't like this any more than Soren did. Once upon a time, they'd been great allies —before he'd taken Bianca as his charl. Guilt ate at him for destroying an important diplomatic friendship.

Wells scanned the room, caught sight of Soren, and scowled.

"You are lucky that he agreed to let you come," Arus said, sidling up next to Soren.

"I know." Soren didn't like to feel leashed, but he had to speak with Wells, and this was his best opportunity. He had to try to make the man understand what he could offer Bianca—immortality and love. She would never want for anything.

"Arus, do you think you can get me an audience with him?" He hated asking, but he was not going to start this battle. He would treat Wells with respect, even if he had to take Bianca away without the man's blessing.

"That was always my intention. You built too much together for me to allow that relationship to end without a fight." Arus walked through the crowd to meet with Wells, speaking to him. Wells shot Soren another look and then nodded, and Arus waved him over. The three of them left the banquet hall and stepped into a small parlor.

"Soren," Wells said coldly.

"President Wells."

For a second neither man spoke, but Soren drew in a breath and tried to relax. "Mr. President, we have worked together for five years to safely and peacefully integrate the Krinar and humans into one society. You and I have both sacrificed much to achieve positive outcomes. There is so much to gain from a continued and growing bond between our peoples."

The president nodded slowly. "I agree. You've surprised me with how much you've stuck to your promise to keep the peace between Ks and humans."

"That's because we are a peaceful race, a race who values love and hard work, especially positive work. We base our value in society on what we bring to others. I have been alive for over eight thousand years."

"Eight thousand?" The president choked on the words. "I knew you lived a long time, but..."

"Yes, and in all that time, I've come to learn how rare it is to find someone who belongs to you, someone who is your other half." He hoped, given what Bianca had said about her mother, that the president would understand the depth of one's feelings for a mate.

"Uh-huh…" The president's eyes narrowed slightly as if he sensed where the conversation was headed.

"What I'm trying to say is that I would like to ask your permission to court Bianca," Soren said. He felt oddly nervous, not because he feared Wells, but the man wasn't his enemy, and he might become family if he would give his blessing. The happiness and fate of their two peoples also rested on this moment. If he and Wells could come to an understanding, especially a positive one, it would make great strides for the peaceful relations between them. Soren didn't want to have to choose between his people and Bianca, even though he knew that if it came down to it, he would choose his charl in a heartbeat above all else.

"My daughter?" Wells drew in a deep breath. "She's too good for you."

"I agree," Soren said immediately. "She's brilliant, compassionate, spirited. She's everything a male dreams of in a charl, or a *wife*." He was careful to add the term that Wells would see as positive. While *charl* was a positive word to the Krinar, it was still seen negatively by humans.

"Wife?" Wells's eyes bulged as he struggled to retain his composure.

"Yes. Those are my intentions. To tie my life to hers in the ways of my people and yours, if she agrees." Of course he knew she would, but her father didn't know that yet.

Arus's surprised gaze drifted between them, and Secret Service agents hovered nervously nearby, as though they expected the president to either attack Soren or have a heart attack.

"I will not"

Wells's cell phone rang, and he stared at the name on it. "It's Bianca." He answered the phone, and then his face went white.

"They want to talk to you." He held up the phone, clearly startled and more than frightened. Soren put it on speaker.

"This is Soren."

A man's gravelly voice came through the phone's speaker. "This is the Anti-K Resistance, Ambassador Soren. We have your human pet. If you want her, she'll be at this address—271 Meadow Lawn Drive, the old tire factory in Princeton."

"What do you want in exchange for her?" Soren held up a hand to silence Wells, who looked ready to shout at the phone.

"What do you *think* we want? For you Ks to leave our planet and never return."

"And if we don't?" Soren challenged, his tone hard-edged. A dark black rage was building inside him. When he found these men, he would rip them limb from limb.

"I will kill her," the man snarled. Wells made a choking sound. Secret Service agents were all whispering urgently into their comms to find the address the man had mentioned.

Soren heard the sound of metal creaking, and then he heard the man speaking to someone else, not him.

"Beg me for your life, traitor." The harsh demand filled Soren with pure terror.

"Go to hell!" Bianca's furious reply came in the background.

"You first, K-loving bitch," the man on the phone snarled.

Bang! The loud pop of a gunshot came through the line, and Wells collapsed into the arms of a quick-moving agent.

Soren roared into the phone, "You will pay for that!" Then it chimed as a live streaming video came through. He stared in horror at the sight of Bianca lying on the ground, clutching her leg. She'd been shot.

"You see that?" the man on the phone snapped. "Get your alien ass here and you can have her, but only after we see you guys getting in your ships and leaving. Try anything dumb, and you can have what's *left* of her."

Arus caught Soren's attention and nodded.

"I will see it done," Soren growled into the phone. The call ended. Soren tossed the phone at Wells. If he hadn't, he would've crushed it into pieces.

"Bianca," Wells moaned. "She can't be…"

"She isn't," Soren said darkly. "She won't be. I'm going to save her."

"You do and you'll have my blessing," Wells said, desperate and afraid. "Please, save my baby girl."

Soren nodded, unable to speak further as he rushed from the room. Arus was right behind him.

"We have a way to fake the ships leaving. I messaged Korum while you were talking. We can broadcast images of our ships taking off like mirages in the skies all over the world. It will look like we are leaving."

"And in the meantime, I can find Bianca and kill every man in my way."

Arus pursed his lips but didn't argue. They rushed from the White House onto the green lawn, where Arus pointed to his waiting ship. It was a large one fully equipped with weapons, a medical bay and sleeping chambers for at least five people.

"We have the location in Princeton. We can be there in five minutes," Arus said.

"Five minutes...I hope she doesn't bleed out by then." He should have given her the nanocytes earlier. He had wanted to wait until she was certain she was ready, and now it might cost her life.

When they arrived minutes later outside the abandoned factory, he gave his cuff to Arus. "Press the groove on the side and you'll be invisible. Use it to watch the outside for me. I don't want to be ambushed inside there."

Arus slipped the cuff on and studied the factory. "Be careful. This is almost certainly a trap. I'll contact you if I see anybody."

Soren's blood pounded through his veins as he stepped toward the entrance of the abandoned factory. The metal doors hung at odd angles on their frames. Just beyond them was darkness broken up by shafts of light from grime-coated windows. Soren listened, straining to hear any sounds. The humans would be stupid to stay here. Once he had Bianca safe, he would hunt them all down and exact his revenge.

"Bianca?" He shouted her name loudly enough that the metal rafters above creaked in protest.

A voice, the same one from the phone call, came over a rusty loudspeaker. "She's on the second floor. Down the hall."

So the humans weren't stupid. They knew better than to be here to face him, but they had set up cameras to monitor his movements. Which meant this *was* a trap. The only question was, what kind? Soren considered the possibilities as he rushed up a flight of narrow stairs and down the hall.

He scanned the halls for choke points and barricades, expecting a legion of armed soldiers hoping to catch him in a crossfire, but he found none. Strange. He carefully avoided debris and the decaying floor tiles as he reached a room with a metal door. He jerked it open, finding the room empty.

"Bi" He grunted as someone threw themselves at him, causing him to shuffle back a step. He was about to retaliate when he realized it was Bianca, who was now limping away from him.

His brave, beautiful charl. She had ripped part of her dress and fashioned a tourniquet over her injured calf.

"Bianca!"

She stopped and turned, mouth agape. "Soren! I thought the man had come back." She threw herself into his arms, burying her face against his chest, her whole body shaking violently.

"Shhh, you're safe now." He cradled her close, trembling with relief just as much as she was. He hadn't wanted to think about what could have happened if he hadn't found her in time.

Bianca suddenly regained control of herself. "We have to go. This is a trap! They're going to blow up the factory!"

Of course. Why didn't he see it sooner? Soren didn't hesitate. He scooped Bianca up in his arms and ran at the same time as he contacted Arus, telling him to find a way to disable the explosives or jam the signal if it was possible. They had made it down the stairs and were halfway across the wide empty space in the main factory floor when that voice spoke once more over the loud-speakers.

"Enjoy hell, alien scum!"

Soren roared as he tried to reach the freedom of the doors. The blast knocked him to the ground and sent Bianca rolling away from him.

The ceiling above them shuddered from the explosion, and he had only seconds to scramble to his feet and throw himself over Bianca, pinning her tightly to the nearest wall as the factory crumbled down all around them.

12

———

Bianca blinked away the dust in her eyes, coughing violently as she tried to move, but she couldn't. She was pinned. By what? Oh right, a building had fallen on top of her. How was she still alive?

The dizzy thought danced around her aching head as she tried to process what had happened. Then her gaze settled on Soren in the suffocating darkness. His body was pressed against hers, crushing her into the floor. Everything hurt, even her eyes.

"Soren..." She shifted an inch, and it cost her so much energy that she went limp, panting for breath in the dark ruins of the factory.

"Soren, are you okay?" She breathed his name, and he stiffened above her.

"No," he rasped. "Not again...can't be trapped..." He panicked, thrashing above her, the rubble still groaning and shifting around them.

She realized he must be remembering his time trapped on Zaruth, waiting to die in the Wailing Pit. The claustrophobia of that experience had to be magnified exponentially right now. She had to find a way to reach through his fear and get him to calm down, or neither of them would make it out of this alive.

Bianca tried to bottle up her own fear and the numbing pain that was slowly spreading through her limbs.

"Soren, it's okay. Listen to me. Just breathe." She was able to get one hand on his chest and caress him in small reassuring strokes. "It's okay. We'll both live. We can breathe. We'll find a way out." She was lying, though. She couldn't breathe. Not enough fresh air was coming in. Dizziness swamped her as she kept trying to focus on him. She couldn't imagine how scared he had to be, trapped again like this.

"Bianca, I can't move. I can't" He grunted, and the debris around them shifted an inch.

"Don't panic," she whispered. "Just breathe..." Her vision turned fuzzy, and she knew she wasn't going to stay conscious for much longer. Tears leaked out of the corners of her eyes. If this was it, there was something she had to say before the end.

"Soren...I love you. Don't forget me if I..." Blackness closed in around her, and her hand fell away from his chest. She thought she heard him roar her name as she fell deeper into a quiet nothingness.

———

SOREN FELT HER HEARTBEAT SLOW AS HER HAND FELL away from him. He closed his eyes, the three hundred years of loss and isolation spurring something other than crippling fear in him. Now it came out in rage. It exploded through him, igniting every fiber of his being until he was pushing back against the debris above, demanding it bow to his will. He roared until his voice was stripped away, and at last the concrete and steel began to succumb. And then the rubble was tumbling to the sides all around him, and he could see the sky and take in fresh air once more. He picked Bianca up, cradling her limp body as he stumbled from the wreckage.

"Soren!" Arus raced over, his face ashen. "We were trying to locate you in the rubble, but something was interfering with our scanners." He nodded at several other Krinar searching the rubble with small hand-held devices, including Sef. "Is there anyone else inside?"

"No," he rasped. "Just us."

Sef joined them. "I felt you...panicking," he whispered and touched his shoulder.

"It was just Zaruth all over again," Soren breathed. "I couldn't get free, but..." He looked down at Bianca, and his blood turned to ice. "She needs medical attention." He stumbled, and Sef caught his arm to steady him.

"Take her, Arus." He offered his friend his charl. Her life was fading, and he was unable to help her. This was far worse than anything he'd ever felt while trapped on Zaruth.

Arus carried her to the ship and laid her down on a bed in the medical bay. Then he began moving a jansha healing device over her. Soren fell to his knees beside the bed, his body hurting like hell. Sef removed his own healing device and began treating Soren.

"Collapsed lungs, gunshot to her calf, broken arm, broken clavicle. A piece of rebar punctured her spine..." Arus looked to him in concern. "If we don't inject her with the nanocytes, she won't survive."

Soren grasped the hand of Bianca's unbroken arm. His eyes burned with tears. Tears he had not shed since those first few moments when he'd climbed from the dark wailing pit on Zaruth and tasted free air again. He had wept like a child then—no, like a man who'd found salvation after believing all was lost. No one had ever seen him like that. Emotionally and physically weak. But Arus was seeing him now, tears streaking down his face, and he was thankful his friend did not judge him.

"She might hate me forever for taking the choice of immortality away from her, but I can't let her die. Inject her." He nodded at Arus, who quickly injected the nanocytes through a slender white tube into Bianca's chest. The nanocytes would be transported quickly through her bloodstream and start healing the grievous wounds faster.

"She's healing—she's taking the nanocytes well," Arus assured him. "I'm sorry, Soren. We should have scanned the building before you went in."

"There wasn't time. We didn't know the extent of her injuries." Soren's words came out soft, but he felt almost wooden, unable to move until he saw her begin to breathe normally.

"I would say she's stable now. She's going to be fine. But we should get her to DC. Her father will need to see her."

Soren moved to lift his female up, ignoring the pain of his own body. He would be fully healed soon.

"I can carry her," Arus offered gently.

"No...thank you, Arus. I need to do it. I'm getting stronger." He was grateful his friend had left him his pride. They left the medical bay on Arus's ship and moved into temporary resting quarters that had a slender bed. Soren laid her down on the bed and used Arus's jansha to aid the healing process as much as possible. When they landed on the front lawn of the White House, Secret Service agents were there waiting for them.

"What's the status of Hummingbird?" one of the men demanded.

"Healing," Soren grunted. Arus pulled the agents aside to debrief them while Soren carried Bianca into the White House. President Wells was waiting inside, and he followed Soren as he carried Bianca to her old bedroom.

"Oh God, Bianca!" Wells gasped. "Let me see her!" He reached for her, but Soren shook his head solemnly.

"Open the door for me. You can see her once she's in her bed. I want her comfortable so she'll heal faster."

Wells opened the door for Soren to enter. It was decorated with antique furniture, but the walls were still covered with posters of her favorite movies and photos of her friends. At least she'd be in familiar surroundings when she woke up.

Soren set her down on the bed and started moving the jansha over her body once more.

"What happened?" Wells demanded.

"The resistance fighters didn't care about us actually leaving. I doubt they ever believed we would leave.

They wanted us dead. The Krinar ambassador and the president's daughter killed together. I believe that would have made a big statement." Soren could now see the moves and countermoves being made by the resistance fighters. His and Bianca's deaths could have caused a severe setback for the peaceful relations between their peoples. Blame could have been thrown in every direction—Krinar, human government, and resistance alike—which was no doubt what they wanted.

"Because you and my daughter..." Wells's face was red now. "You are..." He still couldn't continue.

"Together, despite your orders, and those of my people. I hate to remind you, President Wells, but she is mine. It never mattered what you said, nor did it matter what my own Council said. It only mattered what *she* said. And once she said yes, I would have battled the universe for her." Soren brushed a lock of Bianca's hair back. She made a soft noise and leaned into his touch.

To his surprise, Wells chuckled. "A total eclipse of the heart, eh?"

"What?" Soren was half listening, and the reference was confusing.

"It's an old song by...never mind. Point is, the love you feel for her eclipses everything, right?"

"Yes," Soren agreed, now understanding.

"It was the same for me with her mother. She was

out of my league. Smart, beautiful, compassionate. I was a lovestruck teenager whenever she was around." Wells smiled. But then he met Soren's gaze solemnly. "Tell me, what does this mean for you and my daughter? What life will she have? I don't mean as your companion or pet like many charls are. I want to know, what does she *mean* to you, really?"

Soren considered his words and gazed at Bianca. His heart fluttered as her lips parted and she murmured his name, still asleep.

"She is my eclipse, as you said. There will be nothing I will not give her. There will be nothing I can deny her, either. Friends, her own life, her career. Everything that matters to her now matters infinitely more to me because of our bond." His throat tightened. "I waited so long to find her. My *lilana*."

"*Lilana*?" Wells asked.

"It means soulmate or precious one. She will have all the freedom she wishes, so long as I can be at her side." As he spoke those words, Bianca's eyes opened, and she glanced around, eyes wide with fear.

"Soren, are you okay? How did we get..." Her eyes drifted to her father. "Dad? What are you doing here?"

"Bee, honey, you're back at the White House." Wells smiled at his daughter, and Soren felt a flash of envy for the man and the closeness he had with his daughter. He had known Bianca her entire life, and Soren had only been able to call her his for a few weeks. He reminded himself that he would get the rest of their very long lives to be with her.

"I'm okay, Dad." Bianca moved slightly as her father gently knelt by the bed to hug her. After a moment, they both let go, smiling at each other. Then she leaned into Soren's touch, which made his heart tighten in his chest.

"Is Claudia okay? She was hurt, unconscious when I was kidnapped. Can you go check on her?"

"She's fine. She's at the hospital, but she has a minor concussion. She'll be able to go home tomorrow," Soren explained.

"Thank God, I was so scared for her." Bianca sighed, closing her eyes briefly. Then she looked at Soren with fresh fear. "Soren, there was a woman there...I don't think she was a part of the resistance movement, but I think she hired them. I heard part of their conversation. Her name is Tarah Crowley. She owns a tabloid." Bianca's eyes were clear of pain now, and only a weariness from healing showed in her face.

"Tarah Crowley?" her father snarled. "I should have let the FBI throw the book at her."

"No need," Soren said darkly. "I will handle her. She threatened my people, and we have far more effective and lasting ways to punish someone."

President Wells cleared his throat. "I normally would be concerned upon hearing that, but because of what she did to my daughter, I'll certainly be glad to let you Ks deal with her."

When Bianca tried to sit up, Soren pressed her back into the bed. "Please, rest. You sustained severe injuries, *lilana*. I need you to rest while the nanocytes do their work."

It was the wrong thing to say. Her eyes widened, and she stared at him. "But we were going to wait, Soren. I hadn't...I wasn't ready."

"I'm sorry, *lilana*, but you were dying from your injuries. It was the only way to save you." Soren squeezed her hand, but she pulled away, a look of pain on her face.

"Nanocytes?" Wells asked. "What did you do to her?"

Soren faced the president and then looked at his agents. "Send them outside, and I will tell you."

Wells agreed and sent his security detail outside, and Soren told him about the nanocytes and their immortality benefits.

"So these nano things saved her life?"

Soren answered with a nod.

The president glanced toward his daughter. "Then I'm glad she has them. If I'd been in the same position, I would've made the same call."

Bianca stared at them. "You don't understand. I'll never grow old, but you will."

"I will live out my life as intended. I can accept that, sweetheart."

Soren saw Bianca's eyes fill with tears, and he couldn't bear to see her in such pain.

"Actually, if President Wells makes it clear he welcomes our union, Bianca, I may be able to petition the Council for your father. They recently allowed another human charl's family to be given nanocytes. It's possible they might make an exception for your father once he is out of office and away from the public light."

The blossom of hope in Bianca's eyes made his chest tighten, and she reached for his hand again.

"Thank you," she whispered. He almost forgot her father was right next to him, or he would have tackled her on the bed—gently, of course—and covered her face with kisses.

Wells's eyes were wide, and he looked a little stunned. "Thank you, Soren."

"Don't thank me yet. The Council will have to agree, but if we show them that we are family now, it will strengthen our case."

"I know I promised you my blessing before you left, and you kept your end of the bargain. I stand by my word. But you'll have to marry her in the human way. Public relations, and all that."

"Marriage? Guys, slow down. I'm only twenty-one," Bianca reminded them.

"I will marry her," Soren promised. Bianca huffed, which made Soren chuckle. "When she is ready," he added.

"You had better plan one *heck* of a proposal, buddy," Bianca muttered, but Soren heard a hint of amusement in her voice.

"I will. Once I'm certain you're safe." Ignoring her father, he cupped Bianca's face and kissed her, reminding her of everything they had to look forward to once she was feeling better. When their mouths parted, he relished her dazed, happy look. It was the perfect way to leave her for now. Because he had to go.

He was going to track down the resistance fighters and Tarah Crowley and make sure they could never hurt her again.

———

"YOU'RE SURE ABOUT HIM, BEE?" HER FATHER ASKED after Soren and his brother, Sef, left to track down Tarah Crowley. Bianca was still resting in her bed in the White House, and her father had pulled up an armchair nearby to keep her company.

"More sure than anything in my life," she assured him.

Her father's brows drew together. "You used to be so scared of him, ever since K-Day. You avoided him every chance you had when you were here."

"I thought it was fear of him, but it was fear of the unknown. I *know* him now, I know his heart, his soul. He sees only endless potential in me, and in all humans. He wants to help us, to make us their equals. He has faith in us and faith in me."

"Honey, you *are* his equal. The Krinar aren't better than us. Not when it comes to what lies in our hearts. Yes, they have better technology, but that doesn't mean they have any more nobility and strength of purpose than you do."

Bianca chuckled. "That's not what I meant. I mean I feel like he fits with me. It's not just chemical—it's emotional, even spiritual. When I think about the future, I always see him by my side. He's home to me, a home I've been looking for all my life. I just never knew it until I found him."

Her father cleared his throat, looking away as he blinked away the tears. "A good father wouldn't stand in the way of a man like that."

"I would say a good father would welcome a man like that with open arms, as the son he never had." Bianca curled her fingers around her father's hand. She'd always wondered if her mother's death had left her father feeling that he had missed out on the chance for a son. She had tried to be the best daughter she could, but still the question lingered.

"You know that you're all I've ever wanted and needed, Bee. But I'll be glad to have someone like

Soren as a son-in-law." He suddenly laughed. "Though I can't imagine him wanting to go throw a ball on the front lawn."

Bianca giggled. "Probably not. But maybe he likes golf?"

"You think?" Her father perked up.

"I honestly don't know." She laughed even harder than her father. It helped ease her fears about what dangers Soren might be facing while he was away.

Please be careful. She sent the message out into the universe, hoping he could somehow hear her.

———

TARAH LEANED BACK IN HER DESK CHAIR, GLEEFULLY watching a news report on one of the local stations in New Jersey. Any moment now, the newscaster would mention the breaking story about the bombing of an old tire factory. And thanks to the information she'd fed them, they would put the pieces together and speculate that Ambassador Soren and the president's daughter had been having a torrid love affair and were killed by Krinar terrorists in revenge for their cross-species relationship. By the time the truth was discovered, it wouldn't matter. The damage would be done.

The news station had agreed to pay her well for the story, and the funds should be hitting her bank account at any moment. She retrieved her phone from her desk and opened the banking app. Nothing yet. Might have to wait for the next business day.

A sudden knock on her office door made her curse.

"Go away!" she snapped and focused back on the TV.

A cold, familiar voice frosted the blood in her veins. "Ms. Crowley, I think you're going to want to adjust your tone." She slowly spun around in her chair.

Ambassador Soren and another Krinar who looked exactly like him were standing shoulder to shoulder just inside her office, blocking her escape. She recognized Soren's voice from years of press conferences and political events. But who was the identical man beside him? Did the Ks clone themselves? Maybe Soren was dead and they were both clones of him? This could be a hell of a headline!

Then she remembered she was alone in a room with two of them. Fear prickled inside her like a thousand spiders scuttling beneath her skin.

"I..." She swallowed hard. "What do you want?" She tried to keep her bravado intact, but the blackness of their eyes was terrifying.

"You hired resistance fighters to attack my mate. *Twice.* The little stunt in the factory was *unpleasant*," Soren said as he stepped farther into her office, the panther-like grace of his body spiking her terror even more.

"I don't know what you're talking about. I wasn't even—"

"Enough. We know the truth. Others have talked. You are spiteful and greedy and care nothing about taking a life to get yourself ahead. You're the kind of filth that sets back the future of your people."

She frowned, beaten, but unwilling to yield. "So what are you going to do, kill me?"

Soren loomed over her, his hands pressing at either side of her desk.

"One tiny snap, that's all it would take," he warned in a dangerously gentle tone. He moved fast, catching her neck in his hands, but he didn't squeeze.

"So much for being an enlightened people," she said with a triumphant smirk. "You're no better than us. You're just more dangerous. Just like I've always said." Tarah choked, unable to get air into her lungs as he squeezed. An animal-like panic made her spasm. She flailed, clawing at his hand. Just as her vision began to tunnel, he released her. She fell gasping down to the ground, hitting her knees hard enough that her bones rattled.

"Make no mistake, we are just as capable of violence as you are. But we also know how to afford mercy. You will tell us everything about your connections to the anti-K resistance, and then..." He waited for her to meet his eyes. "Then we will erase your memories. Who you are now will be wiped away forever. But what remains will have a chance to become a better person."

The man who looked like Soren slowly smiled and reached for her. The scream she gave was abruptly cut off.

<h1 style="text-align:center">EPILOGUE</h1>

One month later – Monterey Bay Research Lab

Bianca finished typing up her latest report about sea otters crushing oyster shells on large rock formations along the coast. The shells then bore unique markings from the striking of the shells against the rocks as they sank to the bottom of the sea. The layers of crushed shells could actually be dated back hundreds of years. In a way, the sea otters were leaving an archeological record of their activities, almost like humans would. She hoped the study would change the way the world saw sea otters, as something more than just playful mischief makers.

She shut down her computer and said good night to the two other lab technicians before she slipped off her lab coat and retrieved her purse from her locker. She checked her phone, saw a few text messages from

Claudia and with a little smile, she texted her friend back before putting her phone away.

She walked out of the lab and then froze. Something soft and red lay at her feet. She bent and picked it up. A rose petal? She smoothed her thumb over the velvety surface of the petal and inhaled its soft, alluring scent. She grinned. Lately, she seemed so much more aware of the beauty in life. The scent of a rose, the briny smell of the sea, the heat of Soren's kisses, the sound of children laughing at a park. There were thousands of small joys to be experienced in every moment of the day. After the tire factory, she'd made a promise to herself that if Soren returned to her safe and sound, she would never take anything in life for granted again.

She looked at the petal, wondering how it had gotten into the lab. She glanced around the hall and spotted a second petal farther away. She headed toward it, picking it up too. Then she noticed another petal, and her smile grew even bigger. She started walking down the trail of petals, following the winding maze through the aquarium, laughing sometimes as the trail had her walking around in circles past certain fish exhibits, the ones that were her favorites, naturally. She always paused to look at the brightly colored fish or the elusive octopi or the floating jellyfish. Each moment built up her sense of wonder, but she knew where the trail would ultimately lead.

The kelp forest viewing room.

She drew in a nervous breath as she entered the darkened room, which was lit by sunlight filtering down through the waving strands of kelp. The entire floor of the viewing room was covered in petals. The table had been set up with food, and a tall figure stood with his back to her, but she'd know that form anywhere.

"Soren?" She whispered his name, and he turned around.

"Bianca." He smiled as he walked up to her and held out one hand. Her heart gave a jolt as she placed her palm in his, loving the way they fit together so perfectly. He bent to one knee, and her eyes began to burn with tears. She'd teased him about proposing, and she'd known this moment would someday come, but he'd completely surprised her tonight.

"You are my heart, Bianca. You eclipse everything else in my life. Will you do me the greatest honor of becoming my wife in the human way?"

She laughed a little at his phrase of "the human way," and Soren answered with his own charming smile that made her melt inside.

He removed something from his pocket. Her heart stopped beating when she saw what it was. A ring with a black pearl rather than a gemstone. It was the most beautiful thing she'd ever seen.

"You love the ocean so much, it seemed fitting for you to have a part of its natural treasure."

She stared at it and then at him, her lips quivering.

"Yes." It was the only word that mattered right now. *Yes, yes, yes!*

He swept her into his arms before she could say another word, and he gave her a kiss full of honey and fire. He caught her left hand and slipped the ring onto her finger, but she could only think of the endless, glorious future which lay ahead of them.

When their mouths parted, he held her close, their foreheads touching.

"The Council granted my request for your father. He will be given the nanocytes after his term as president is over. The Council has decided that your father will become an ambassador of Earth when he finishes his last term, and he will live among my people in a Krinar Center as part of a cultural exchange. It will help cover the fact that he will start to de-age rapidly. We can visit him as often as you like. The nearest center is an hour from here."

Bianca's head was still buzzing with joy as she gazed into her lover's face. How had she ever feared this man? His brown eyes were as warm as honey, and concern lined his face as he studied her in return.

"I wish..."

"Yes?" he asked.

"I wish you knew how much I love you. How it fills

me inside with such joy that I feel I might start crying." She couldn't stop a sniffle from escaping. "You're the most wonderful man." She laughed and wiped at her eyes. "I just wish you could feel what is inside me."

"I think I do, Bianca." He nuzzled her, smiling softly. "When I struggled from the Wailing Pit to freedom, I fell to my knees and wept like a child because of the joy of being free and alive. Holding you now in my arms is a thousand times stronger than that moment."

He bent his head toward hers and kissed her again. The scent of roses and the flickering sunlight filtering through the kelp created a private nirvana for them, a heaven of their own making. Soren was right. Their love for each other was an eclipse. A Krinar eclipse.

SEF STARED INTO THE BATHROOM MIRROR. GONE WERE his dark-brown eyes and russet hair. Now he had dark-blond hair and blue eyes. These were features not found naturally in Krinar. He looked like a human, but a human version of himself. It was unsettling. Very unsettling. But his skin was still a deep golden tan color, which was human enough.

He rubbed a hand over his jaw as he gave himself one more look in the mirror before he slung his leather motorcycle jacket on. He hadn't cared for the feel of animal skin at first, but he'd grown to accept it. Still, he looked forward to the day where he could be himself and not a Krinar guardian constantly trying to root out the last of the human resistance.

Stepping out of the bathroom at the truck stop in Kansas, he eyed the humans nearby. No Krinar here. The resistance was strongest in middle America, primarily because the Krinar had stopped the production of animals for meat and dairy products. The farmers had been ordered to start growing fruits and vegetables instead, but many had not been able to make the change effectively. The heart of the businesses here in the Midwest, as humans called it, had been drastically affected. Sef knew about the situation, but his job wasn't to change the economy. His duty was strictly in law enforcement and espionage. As a guardian, he was duty bound to protect his people, and even the humans from themselves, if necessary.

He nodded politely at the convenience store clerk. The man offered a friendly nod back. Once outside, Sef climbed into the 1967 black Mustang that he'd created using his fabricator. He curled his fingers around the black steering wheel and studied the horizon. The flat plains of Kansas were glowing with the setting sun. A sign beside the road read, "Lawrence, Kansas—2 Miles."

He knew what he would find once he got there. A small bar run by two brothers, Liam and Mason King. They were leaders of an anti-K resistance movement, and Sef was going to infiltrate them, find out what level of threat he was dealing with, and neutralize them.

They would never see him coming.

THANK YOU SO MUCH FOR READING *THE KRINAR ECLIPSE*! If you want to see how Sef, Soren's twin brother, gets tamed by a human female, keep reading for a 3 chapter sneak peek of *The Krinar Code* by Emma Castle!

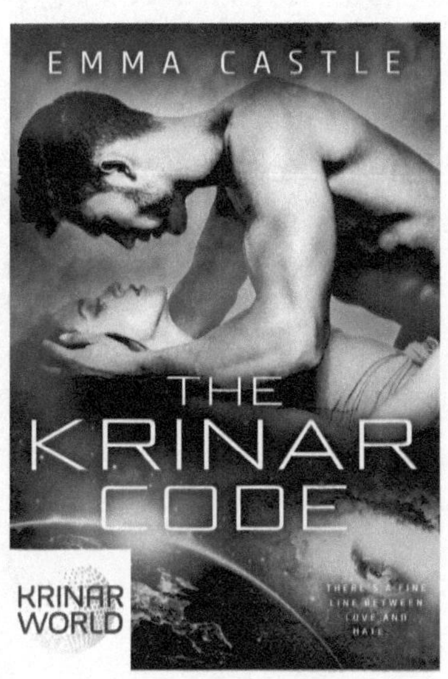

BEFORE YOU TURN THE PAGE...

The best way to know when a new book is released is to do one or all of the following:

Join my Newsletter: http://laurensmithbooks.com/free-books-and-newsletter/

Follow Me on BookBub: https://www.bookbub.com/authors/lauren-smith

Join my Facebook VIP Reader Group called Lauren Smith's League: https://www.facebook.com/groups/400377546765661/

Now…turn the page to see what sexy trouble Sef can get into in *The Krinar Code*!

THE KRINAR CODE BY EMMA CASTLE

CHAPTER 1

"Ow!" Harper King swallowed a curse as she sucked on her pinched thumb. The big Corvette suspended above her was in decent shape, but the axle was dented all to hell. The owner had been pissed when she'd recommended he replace the axle or sell the car. Given that it was an expensive classic, he'd opted for the replacement, but he'd grumbled the entire time. Between the parts and labor to fix them, new axles could cost almost as much as the car itself. She didn't mind the work, but the customers at King Auto Repair usually didn't like the price.

"You okay, Harper?" A deep voice came from nearby. She glanced around and saw her older brother's boots as he stopped next to the car she was beneath.

"Yeah, I'm fine, Mason." She lay flat on her creeper

and pushed herself so she rolled out from underneath the Corvette. Her thumb still stung from where it had gotten caught in part of the undercarriage. She glowered at the car. "This axle, though, is going to have a very bad day tomorrow." She tilted her left wrist to check her watch. It was a little after nine at night, and her brother should have been working, not here in the garage.

Mason held out a hand, his brown eyes full of worry. He and Liam didn't approve of her running the mechanic shop on her own, but she was damned good at it, and they needed to get with the century.

Mason's eyes darkened with shadows, and his voice lowered. "Liam and I have a meeting tonight. You got any more jobs, or can you watch the bar with Neil for the rest of the night?"

She let Mason lift her up onto her feet, and she glanced around at the shop. "Yeah, I can watch it for you." She didn't mind tending bar most of the time, but her true love was the auto shop.

King Auto Repair shared a building with King's Bar, the bar that her brothers ran together. It wasn't much, but given that Lawrence, Kansas, was a little college town of just under a hundred thousand people, it passed for the center of the local nightlife.

Harper wiped at the sweat on her brow. It was quiet. The usual sounds of electric drills, men whistling, car hoods slamming, and the symphony of choking engines, sputtering motors, and hydraulic ramps going up and down were absent since they'd closed two hours ago. Her two employees, Jeff and Alan, had already left for the day. The shop had closed at seven, and she'd been so deep into her work that she'd lost track of time. It wasn't the first time that had happened. When she was working, she could dive so deep into the job that the rest of the world just fell away.

"You and Liam will be careful, won't you?" she asked him.

Mason, at twenty-nine, and Liam, at thirty-one, were grown men, but Harper still worried about them. Ever since they had lost their parents on K-Day, the day the Krinar invaded Earth, the three of them seemed to be standing alone against the world.

"We'll be fine," Mason promised her. He and Liam wouldn't let her join their meetings because they thought it was too dangerous for her. They were running a resistance group out of the back of the bar. Every couple of weeks they held a meeting with local men and women who wanted to find a way to resist the Krinar occupation. But even if they had let her join, she wouldn't have. Humans couldn't fight the Krinar— or the Ks, as most humans called them—and it was just out of plain old human stubbornness that they even tried.

From the moment they had arrived five years ago,

the aliens had taken charge, almost effortlessly. They looked human enough, just insanely attractive, like muscled supermodels. They weren't skinny and gray with black oval eyes like many people obsessed with extraterrestrials had expected them to be, and they sure as shit didn't need help phoning home like E.T. The Krinar were stronger, faster, and smarter than humans. They lived for thousands of years and had technology that made Earth science look like humans were still banging rocks together trying to make fire.

We never stood a chance when they invaded. What makes anyone think we have one now?

Harper sighed and rubbed her grease-covered hands on a towel and watched Mason walk back through the hall that connected the bar to the garage. Then she busied herself with closing down the shop. She made a note in her calendar to call the Corvette owner tomorrow with an update, but the simple task of writing tended to make her head hurt.

She'd been diagnosed with severe dyslexia in high school. She'd graduated high school, barely, but she hadn't been able to get into college. Numbers were easier to write, but words and names? It was like she was watching the letters dance around the page, and it gave her a migraine. If her father hadn't discovered she had a knack for mechanics, she didn't know where she might have ended up.

Thankfully, engines, mechanics, and electronics all

came to her with stunning clarity. When she'd turned eighteen, she'd been able to take over her father's repair shop.

Harper paused to look at the photo of her parents that hung behind the reception desk inside the shop. In the photo her parents were standing outside the repair shop entrance. It had been taken nearly twenty years ago when she was only four. Her father beamed with pride, and her mother was looking at him with admiration. They'd been so in love, so in tune with one another.

And they were gone.

A deep sting lanced through Harper's chest, a pain of loss and sorrow that would never fully heal, no matter how much time had passed. No one deserved to die the way they had.

She kissed the tips of her fingers and pressed them to the glass of the framed photo. "Night, Mom and Dad."

Then she lowered the shop doors, set the alarm system, turned off the lights, and passed through the hall and into the small office between the auto shop and the bar. The large desk against the far wall by the single window was littered with paperwork from both the shop and the bar. Harper growled. Every night she came back here she had to clean up after Mason and Liam. They were great at dealing with vendors and customers, but they sucked at basic business organization and bookkeeping. She practically had to pester them to keep up their records.

Harper shoved the papers aside to retrieve the folded set of clean clothes she brought to work every day. Shop work always left her khaki work suit covered in grease. She changed into her jean shorts and T-shirt with the King's Bar logo, a retro-looking crown beneath the King name in a bold stylistic font. Then she removed her work boots and slipped on some simple leather sandals. She wasn't girly, not compared to most girls she knew, but after work she did like to feel a bit more feminine, even if she was tending bar for her older brothers.

As she exited the office, she could hear the rowdy sounds of the bar over the thrumming bass of the bar's modern jukebox. She opened the door and scanned the room. The walnut wood tables and even the bar itself were full, which was typical for a Saturday night. The kids from the University of Kansas loved to come and hang out after tough classes all week.

"Harper!" Jessie Lang, one of the full-time waitresses, grinned and waved at Harper. Jessie carried a full tray of beers toward a table of men who were watching the nearest flat-screen TV hanging from one of the bar's support beams. They whooped as someone made a touchdown. College football was serious business in Kansas, and any good bar worth its salt would have a dozen TVs up and running with the latest games on.

Harper smiled and waved at Jessie as they shared an amused shrug at the men talking football stats. She and Jessie were close in age, and she usually spent her free weekends hanging out with Jessie.

A lot had changed since the Krinar had arrived. They had shut down production of beef and poultry, for one thing. Enforced veganism, most people called it, and she had to admit, of all the jackbooted declarations she had expected to come down the pipe from their new overlords, that was pretty damn close to the bottom of the list.

But it had hit the Midwest hard. Many cities became ghost towns, and people had moved away and sold their grazing fields, which were unsuitable for crops and were now empty and valueless. It was why so much resistance had formed here against the Krinar. Mason and Liam had mobilized their friends who'd lost work when their homes had been sucked into the economic black hole the Krinar invasion had created. And their friends had brought other friends, and so on.

All because those damn aliens didn't eat meat.

If I ever meet one of them, I'll shove a cheeseburger right down their throat. The rebellious thought made her smile widen. Having to eat the plant-based protein burger patties made her gag.

"How's it going?" she asked her friend as she joined her at the bar.

Jessie laughed, her dark-brown eyes bright with her natural joy. "Busy as hell, and Katie's got the flu. You mind taking orders from those tables in the corner?" Jessie reached across the bar, where she placed a new drinks order ticket for their bartender, Neil, who was busy mixing.

"Sure." Harper gave Neil a nod, and he flexed his tattooed arms as he shook the martini mixer. The wall behind him was covered with a hundred bottles of decent liquor, as well as some more expensive scotch and brandy. People came from miles around to King's Bar—students, farmers, blue-collar workers, and even some upper-middle-class folk. Her parents had left a legacy of openness and welcoming to all. Harper could gripe about a lot of things with regard to her older brothers, but they were great at keeping the bar fun, except on nights they hosted resistance meetings in the back storeroom. Those always made her nervous.

Harper bit her lip and glanced toward the *Employees Only* sign hanging on the door. The closely spaced letters jumbled about and made her grimace. She'd tried to develop her own shorthand to work with Neil when giving him orders, but it still was a challenge.

"Sure, Jessie. I'll cover the two tables in the back corner." She picked up a pen and notepad from the bar, her stomach cramping at the thought of having to write down drink orders.

She reached the first table, where a tall man lounged back in his chair, watching the room. His blue eyes swept to her face as she approached, and Harper's heart jolted as she felt the full focus of his stormy blue gaze. Damn, the man was fine. *More* than fine. He had long legs and narrow hips, but he also had those broad shoulders all women loved. His red plaid shirt hung open to reveal a gray T-shirt underneath that clung a little too snug to his skin, which hinted at a hard chest and chiseled abs.

Wow. Where had this hunk of man meat come from? Harper blushed and stared at her sandals. It was not okay to objectify a guy, right? She was a total feminist—she had to be around her overprotective brothers. But damn if this guy didn't make her want to wolf-whistle.

Harper finally looked at the man before her again, and that was a mistake. "W-what can I get you?"

His golden-blond hair fell into his eyes, and he casually brushed it back. How could such a simple gesture make her knees buckle? The sleeves of his shirt were rolled up to his elbows, exposing the muscles of his forearms. Harper swallowed hard. Damn again— she was having a serious attraction to this complete stranger. Something that was totally not like her. She usually kept to herself these days. She'd dated a lot in the past, sure, but lately she'd been so focused on work she'd lost track.

"I'll take an India Pale Ale. Whatever kind you recommend. Thanks." His lips curved in a telltale bad-boy smile that scared her shitless. It was a smile that promised nothing but broken hearts. An IPA, that was easy enough to remember. She lowered her notepad in relief, not bothering to write that order down. She started to head back to the bar to grab his drink, but as she passed by the next table, a man grabbed her arm.

"Not so fast, sweetheart. We need drinks too. We've been here ten minutes already."

Harper gritted her teeth. She didn't mind being called *sweetheart* by a boyfriend, but by some tool like this? She eyed the rough-looking man, and his friends all snickered at her open discomfort. She wanted to flip them off, but that wasn't going to help. She plastered on a reluctant smile and lifted her pad up.

"What can I get you?" *And by that I mean, "What can I have Neil spit in?"*

The men all started throwing exotic drink orders at her, and she struggled, frantically penning down their orders, but within seconds the panic set in. Her pen froze, and she closed her eyes briefly.

"What's the matter with you? Why aren't you writing our orders down?" the first asshole demanded.

"I am!" she snapped. "I just need a minute. I" She turned again to list the drinks, but she couldn't correctly spell some of the more complicated orders, and then it was too late. The letters began to almost quiver on the page, and she suddenly couldn't decipher her own writing.

"You stupid or something?" one of the men asked her. His companions broke out into more laughter.

Harper grabbed the nearest water glass and threw its contents into the face of the man who'd called her stupid. He surged to his feet and backhanded her so fast she never saw the blow coming.

Pain ripped through her and she stumbled back, clutching her face in shock. A hush settled over the crowd, and Harper shot a glare at the man. She wasn't afraid to throw a punch, but she was outnumbered. And with her luck, she'd break her hand on his jaw.

"You have a problem?" the man who'd struck her now snapped at her.

"Out! I want you and your asshole buddies out of here!" Harper yelled. While this wasn't technically her bar, she felt like a part owner of it, the same way her brothers felt about her garage. And like the sign over the bar said, "*We reserve the right to refuse service to anyone who's an asshole.*"

"Oh yeah?" The man spread his arms out wide, noting the lack of security coming to restrain him. Normally Neil would have been right there, kicking this guy's ass, but he'd broken his leg last week on his motorcycle and was stuck on crutches behind the bar. "Who's gonna make me?"

"Pardon me," a deep masculine voice said right behind her as two large hands settled on her waist. She was lifted up and set aside by the gorgeous blond Adonis from the other table.

"I believe the lady asked you to leave. And your asshole buddies."

The asshole and his friends all stood. Six to one—those weren't good odds. "Is that so?"

"That's so."

"Hey, you really don't need to" Harper touched the Adonis's rock-hard shoulder.

The Adonis swung a fist fast, almost too fast to see. It connected with the asshole's jaw, and he stumbled back, knocking over three chairs, and his head collided with the wall in a heavy *thunk*. He didn't stir. One of his friends knelt down to check his pulse.

"Chase is out cold," the other man said. They all turned to face the Adonis again.

"I suggest you get out. Now. And take your trash with you," Adonis growled in a tone that sent shivers of dread through Harper. She'd seen plenty of men try to fake being a badass over the years, but this guy wasn't faking. He was dangerous. *Really* dangerous. And he'd just saved her ass.

The group of jerks rushed out of the bar, only two of them stopping to lift Chase up and carry him out.

Neil followed them to the door on his crutches, scowling the entire way. Adonis watched them go, his arms crossed. Once they were gone, the conversations in the bar went back to normal, and the stares of curious bargoers eventually drifted away from them.

"Are you all right?" The man cupped her chin as he tilted her face toward his, checking where she'd been struck. A flare of warmth seeped from his palm into her skin, and she tried not to shiver at the feminine awareness of him that made her shyly try to step away.

"He got me pretty good, but I'll be okay." She needed to escape the heat of his gentle touch. The man was gorgeous, but in a purely masculine way. A blush spread over her face, and her right cheek throbbed hotly with the added rush of blood.

"You'll need to ice your cheek, or it's going to swell and bruise. Come." He caught her hand and started pulling her along behind him toward the bar. Too stunned to object, she followed along.

"Oh my God, Harper!" Jessie met them at the bar, along with Neil. "Should I get Mason and Liam?"

Jessie's gaze darted to Adonis, and she choked down whatever else she might have said next. She just blinked in a dazed way that Harper completely understood. This man was just the kind of perfect male specimen that would leave any girl gobsmacked.

"I'm okay, Jessie. Mr....er...what's your name?" Harper asked.

"Seth Jackson. Call me Seth." His stormy blue eyes were still filled with concern.

"Thank you, Seth. Why don't you go back to your table, and I'll get your…IPA, wasn't it? On the house."

"Thank you. But first I want to make sure you are all right." His lips slid into a slow smile that only intensified her blush. Seth looked toward Jessie. "Can you get me some ice, please?"

"Yeah, sure, hang on." Jessie retrieved the ice and a towel and handed them to Seth.

"Sit," he ordered. Harper found herself gently but firmly planted on a barstool. He wrapped the bagged ice in the towel and put it to her bruised cheek. She reached up, expecting him to let her take over, but their hands touched when she tried to hold the ice up. An electric pulse jumped between them, and her body seemed to hum inside from the connection.

Wow. She was turned on just being close to him. The ice had already started to soak the towel and drip down her arm and his. She was captivated by him and the way his gaze seemed to swallow her up, leaving her mind free of thoughts and instead focused only on sensations.

"Thanks. I think I've got it now," she managed to say, embarrassed by how breathless she sounded.

"Okay, but I'm going to stay here and keep an eye on you. You might have a concussion." He held out his hand. "Let me take your pad. I can get orders for you."

"No!" she almost yelped. She did not want him to see her hastily scribbled and disjointed words. "I mean, thanks, but I'll be fine."

"Harper, he's right, I shouldn't have asked you to take orders. Not with your"

"Jessie!" She cut her friend off. She didn't like people knowing about her dyslexia. It was a common enough condition, but there were always people who didn't understand and who gave her funny looks or treated her differently when they found out. She did not want Seth to look at her like that.

Because I'm not broken, dammit.

She had to remind herself of that. Having severe dyslexia did not mean that she was damaged or not smart. Quite the opposite. People with dyslexia actually absorbed too much information at once, and while that made reading difficult, it did enhance her awareness of more details than the average person, especially visually. It made her one heck of a mechanic. She could rebuild practically anything mechanical from scratch, all by instinct.

"Seriously, go, I'm fine. I'll bring you your drink in a moment." She tried to wave him off, but Seth just grinned.

"You're bossy, but cute as a button. I'm not going anywhere, and neither are you. Keep your butt in that chair." He held out a hand to Jessie. "Give me a pad and tell me which tables need orders."

Jessie gave Harper an apologetic look as she gave a spare pad and pen to Seth.

"Just three tables near the door. We should be good unless someone waves you over."

"Got it." Seth headed over to a table, his back to Harper as he talked to the men and women there.

"Damn, that ass is tight enough to bounce a quarter off of." Jessie giggled and nudged Harper, who was staring at it too. He filled out those blue jeans nicely.

"You need to hit that tonight," Jessie said as she loaded a tray with a couple of margaritas.

Harper rolled her eyes and adjusted the bag of ice against her cheek. Her fingers were a little chilly but not frozen.

"I'm not tapping anything," she muttered. "Not tonight, anyway."

"Pity. He looks like he wants to eat you up...or eat you out." Jessie was giggling again.

"Get your mind out of the gutter."

"Girl, it never left." Jessie's brown eyes twinkled before she trotted off to deliver the margaritas to a waiting table.

Harper watched Seth take more orders, and she sighed. God, she would love to sleep with a guy like that, but she was done with the whole dating-sexy-guys thing. It didn't end well. Her last boyfriend, Xander, had been too cute for his own good, and he knew it.

Eventually his hands had wandered off, and the rest of him had followed. Harper had gone home to their shared apartment the night of their one-year anniversary and spent two hours baking and cooking for their dinner. By ten p.m. she'd finally blown out the candles, removed her black high heels and her sexy little red dress, and put the food in the fridge. It had been obvious he'd forgotten and wasn't coming.

She'd crawled into bed and cried so much she'd smeared mascara all over her pillowcase. The next morning, she'd called him and he'd apologized, and then she'd heard the other woman's voice in the background asking who it was.

She'd never trusted any good-looking man after that, and if she was being truly honest, she didn't trust *any* man fully after that. It wasn't in her nature to leave herself so vulnerable, but Xander had made her want to trust him, and their chemistry had been so good that she'd let her hormones make all the decisions.

Still, she wasn't opposed to dating or even casual sex with nice, normal guys. But a man like Seth? No. He was trouble. She was done with guys like him for sure. They were too easy to fall for, and she was done with being a sucker for a good-looking guy. Seth was trouble, and she was going to stay the hell away from him.

CHAPTER 2

The mission was in jeopardy.

Sef was supposed to be keeping a low profile, posing as "Seth," a human male ready to join the resistance that the King brothers, Mason and Liam, were running out of the back of the bar. Instead, he was taking drink orders after having almost killed a human who'd struck their sister, Harper, the curvy little human with sweet eyes and a scent that made him want to growl with longing. He was lucky he had pulled his punch; otherwise, he would've crushed the man's jaw and possibly killed the bastard. Though he probably deserved it, that would have created even more complications for the mission.

Focus on being calm. She's okay. The idiots are gone. She's safe.

If there was one thing he hated, it was violence

toward a female. From the moment Harper King had walked up to his table, he'd caught her sweet feminine scent untarnished by heavy perfumes and had gotten hard fast. She was definitely his type. Small, curvy, and feisty. But she was off-limits.

Normally when he saw a female he wanted, he would seduce her, with her willing cooperation, and then fuck her for a week straight until he'd gotten her out of his system. But if he did that with Harper, it risked his ability to earn the trust of her brothers. For now he would have to play the gentleman, to use a phrase he'd picked up recently. But damned if the little female didn't tempt him almost beyond reason and control.

As a Krinar male, he could claim her as a charl, which was the Krinar term for a human companion, but he had never taken a charl. It was too lasting, too intimate of a relationship. He was eight thousand years old, and while he'd had hundreds of lovers over the years, he had never chosen to be a cheren to any of them. He wasn't so foolish and impulsive as his twin brother, Soren. Taking a charl would be permanent. Any human taken as a charl would be given nanocytes, which would extend their lives indefinitely at peak age and peak condition, keeping them forever young. Sef had never considered any female he'd met to be someone he would share forever with, but Harper

King was making his mind and desires stray into dangerous territory.

How had this human so suddenly captivated him? Perhaps he was getting soft spending so much time on Earth. Or maybe it was the fact that Soren had recently taken a human charl, and through their shared bond he was sensing such feelings of contentment that it made him long for a charl of his own.

If that was the case, he was going to punch his brother the next time he saw him. Such feelings of desire, sentimentality, and intimacy were harmful to his mission.

He zoned out, writing down drink orders and waiting patiently for the humans to finish ordering. Then he walked back to the bar and slipped the bartender the order.

"Thanks, man. We appreciate the help tonight. I'm Neil." The bartender held out his hand over the polished walnut counter.

Sef slapped his palm into the other man's. He seemed strong, for a human. "Seth Jackson. Happy to help."

"Thanks for saving the kid. Harper's sweet. If I'd been closer and not dragged down with these damn crutches, I would've done exactly what you did and thrown out that trash."

Sef nodded and smiled, but a flicker of a strange emotion shot through him as Neil called Harper sweet.

For one split second he imagined punching Neil and breaking his jaw.

Was he jealous? Over a human female? If Soren ever found out, he would never live it down. Soren was the Krinar ambassador to Earth, and he had recently done a very human thing and gotten engaged to the American president's daughter, Bianca Wells.

Sef glimpsed his reflection in the glass behind the bar and for a second didn't recognize himself. Despite the fact that Sef had left for this mission a few days ago, he still hadn't gotten used to how his looks had changed for this mission. Like all Krinar, he had brown eyes and brown hair, though his was a little more russet, a color unique to his family and their region of their planet, Krina. But for this mission he had been given contact lenses and a hair treatment to turn his hair a golden blond.

Humans wouldn't suspect him to be Krinar so long as he kept his super-strength and increased speed hidden from them. That was why striking that bastard who'd hit Harper tonight had been so dangerous. Sef had almost blown his cover just by punching him. But after seeing Harper hit, he'd nearly lost his mind.

There was something about her that called to him and played upon his protective instincts. He didn't like the way just looking at her made his blood hum and his body ache for dark pleasures. Already he wanted to sink his teeth into her neck and taste her blood. The high it would give them both would be unbelievable. But he had to hold back. He needed to stay undercover, and the last thing he needed was to perpetuate the rumors that Ks were blood drinkers. They were, of course, but his people wished to keep that quiet for now.

Sef spent the next two hours helping Jessie and Neil manage the bar before it was finally closing time. Harper's face was still a nasty shade of red, and he examined it while Neil cleaned the bar and Jessie tidied up the tables.

"I'm fine." She blushed and tried to push his hand away. He didn't like it when she pulled away from him, but given his height and build, it was understandable that a small female like Harper would be wary of him at first. He had no such problems with Krinar females, but at that moment only one female mattered, and she was human.

"Honey, you aren't fine. That asshole landed one hell of a blow." In order to soothe her, Sef slipped into the more casual words and phrases he'd learned. It was one of the many talents that made him such a good guardian for undercover operations.

Harper winced. "If he hadn't had all his friends with him, I would've taken him out." The conviction of her statement confused him.

"You would *date* that man?"

Now Harper was confused. "No, *take out*. Beat to a pulp. Taken out on a stretcher."

Sef chuckled. "Oh, of course. Adorable and blood-thirsty. Are you trying to drive me crazy?" he muttered.

"Huh?" Harper blinked and stared at him.

"Hey, Seth?" Neil called out. "Come meet the bosses." Neil nodded at the *Employees Only* door. Two tall human males, almost as tall as him, came out through the door as it swung open. They looked similar to Harper, but where she was small and feminine, they were tall and masculine, decent specimens of human males. Krinar females would be attracted to these two if they ever visited an X-club or a Krinar Center.

"Mason, Liam," Neil called out, and pointed at Sef with his thumb. "This guy saved little Harper's ass a while ago."

"I didn't need saving." Harper's adorable grumble went unheard by all but him. The Krinar had heightened senses, including hearing.

"What happened?" Liam asked. He and Mason came over to Harper by the edge of the bar.

"Some asshole slapped me," Harper admitted, shame coloring her tone. "Caught me off guard."

Neil finished the story. "Seth here knocked him out cold with one punch and sent his friends packing. They had to carry the guy out."

"Jesus, Harper, come get us next time." Mason tried to look at Harper's face, but she turned away, annoyed.

"Hey, thanks, man." Liam offered a hand. "Seth, was it?"

Sef took it, then shook Mason's as well. "Seth Jackson. You're welcome. No one hits a woman on my watch." *And I would have killed the bastard if there hadn't been any witnesses,* he added silently.

"What can we do to make it up to you?" Liam offered.

And this was what made his risky action tonight worthwhile. He had hoped to ingratiate himself to the King brothers somehow, and this was a perfect opportunity.

"Actually, I'm passing through, but I could use a job. Maybe a recommendation of where to stay? I'll be around a couple of months." He hoped the brothers would offer him a way to stay close until he could infiltrate their operation.

"He was pretty helpful tonight," Jessie volunteered. "We were down a waitress, and he was great."

"Oh?" Liam glanced at Neil and Harper, who both nodded in agreement. "Well...would you like that? We pay a few bucks above minimum wage, and any tips you make are entirely yours."

"Thanks. That would be great." Sef grinned and noticed Harper shoot him a glance. He wished he could read her thoughts. Her expressions were so guarded.

"We even have a spare room in the apartment next

door. Harper lives on the first floor. You could have the room on the second floor if you're interested. It needs some work, but we would only charge two hundred a month."

"Sounds like my lucky day. I can afford that." Sef could afford whatever he needed, but he was here to play the role of a human drifter, moving from town to town. The King brothers weren't idiots—it would take time to win their trust and convince them to let him join their movement.

"Harper, why don't you get him a bar T-shirt for work and show him the apartment. We can handle the paperwork tomorrow," Mason suggested.

Harper blew out a little breath but didn't argue. "This way." She led him to a door that connected to the auto shop. There was an office in the small space between the two businesses but it was separated by a door to give it privacy. Harper opened a large cardboard box beside the desk and shot a glance at him, sizing him up.

"XL, I assume?" she asked before turning back to the box.

"Yeah." He stared at her curvy ass as she bent over, and he licked his lips, unable to stop imagining how it would feel to bend her over the table and pound that soft little bottom, listening to her scream his name in pleasure.

No. Off-limits. Could blow everything.

She straightened and faced him, holding a King's Bar T-shirt. He took it and studied the crown logo.

"King's, huh? You need a shirt that says Queen's as well."

Harper's eyes brightened, and she suddenly smiled. "My dad used to call my mom Queenie. She loved that."

"Did something happen to them?" he asked.

He already knew they were dead. During the Great Panic that had followed the day his people had invaded, many humans had died. The chaos had been hard to prevent. Soren, his brother, had done much to quell fears and resistance early on by working with the human president here in the United States, but there was still violence, riots and deaths that had been unavoidable—and very one-sided. Even with the Coexistence Treaty in place, there were still anti-K groups and all the dangers that came with that.

"They died during the Great Panic. They were on a bridge in their car. Someone blew up the bridge, thinking it would hurt the Ks, but all it did was kill forty-three innocent people, all humans. They were trapped, drowned. They never even found my mother's body." Her voice roughened, and she wrapped her arms around herself, as though she needed a hug.

Sef hated to think that innocent humans had suffered because of them. His people didn't want to hurt anyone. They wanted to—*needed* to—live peacefully alongside them, but until humans learned to accept that their world had changed, his people had to retain control.

And it wasn't like they had been terribly good custodians before the Krinar had arrived. Between pollution and overpopulation, this world needed their protection in order to survive. Sef's people needed Earth because their own sun was dying. They had only a few thousand years to make Earth stable before they could bring the rest of the Krinar here. Which meant the humans needed to learn to share. And though they didn't know it yet, the humans owed their very existence to the Krinar.

"Thanks for the shirt," he said. "I'm sorry about your parents." He paused, holding his breath. "Do you hate them? The Ks, I mean?"

Harper's gaze shifted to a distant look, and her mouth hardened.

"*Hate* is such a strong word. I don't *hate* them. But I want them to leave. They've ruined so much, especially here. Middle America is dying. They want us to grow fruits and vegetables, but some people need meat protein in their diets, and not all farmlands have the right soil to be turned from grazing fields into crop-yielding land. Not to mention it's a bit off-putting being told what to do. Un-American, you might say."

Sef smirked at that. Stubbornness was a trait one could apply to this nation.

"Our way of life was taken away, and we didn't get any say in how to stay alive. It's one thing to have lofty ideals and to force people to bend to your will and all that, but if you don't stop to look at how it impacts others, doesn't that make *you* a monster? The Ks were wrong to do what they did. This is *our* home. We live, fight, and die on this little blue planet. The Ks could go somewhere else if they can't respect us and our lives here. They have the technology to travel anywhere—I've seen it."

"You have?" That surprised him. His files on the King family hadn't suggested she'd encountered any Krinar up close.

"I mean, not in person, but I've seen pictures and videos." Suddenly Harper's eyes were bright with excitement. "They're all close-lipped about what they can do, but FTL, or faster-than-light travel, is no small feat. Plus we know they have special healing devices, and..." She blushed again and cleared her throat. "Sorry, don't get me started talking about Krinar technology. But I'd give a small fortune to be able to take apart even one of their children's toys for ten minutes." She grabbed a set of keys hanging from a hook on the wall and left the office. Sef followed behind, and she led him through the darkened garage and out another door. He wanted to know more about what she thought about Krinar technology, but it was wise to keep his mouth shut.

"The apartment building connects to the far end of my shop."

"*Your* shop?" He'd assumed her brothers also owned the auto shop. He'd only glanced at her dossier before he'd come here. She wasn't his target, after all.

"Yep. Brothers got the bar; I got the garage. I'm good with machines, always have been. Dad let me take over after I graduated high school."

"No college?"

"No—self-taught. So what? Bill Gates never graduated either." He smelled a faint trace of panic in the air just as he had back in the bar when he'd asked her to give him her notepad. She'd refused. There was something there that bothered him, but he couldn't figure out what.

"So, there's another door outside you can get in if you want." She opened the door from the auto shop to a stairwell and held up a ring with a green fob. "This key with the green fob opens the outside door to the stairs, and the red fob opens your apartment. It's that one up there." She nodded up the stairs. He trailed behind her as she led him to the apartment.

The room was dark and musty as he searched for a light switch. There was a small kitchen, a bedroom, and a little living room. Adequate, if a bit small for his tastes.

"I'll grab some fresh bed linens. We keep the mattress bare until we rent the room." She went to the linen closet by the bedroom and pulled out some sheets. "I washed these a few days ago. The fridge is empty, but there's a supermarket just a block away. Only it's not open right now. Have you had dinner?"

Sef shook his head. He wasn't terribly hungry, but if she was offering to cook, he'd be more than happy to accept—to protect his cover, of course.

"Why don't you get settled and come down to my apartment when you're done. I'll whip something up. I always end up having a late dinner on nights like these."

He watched her walk away, unable to deny the sway of her bottom in those jean shorts. When she shut the door behind her, he gave his head a little shake and focused on fixing up his bedding. He then removed a small device from his pocket and sent an encrypted message to Arus, one of his friends, who was also a powerful and influential Krinar. Arus was the one who'd given him this mission.

Sef: *I've made contact with the King brothers and have a job at their bar as well as living accommodations nearby. My next goal is to gain their trust and show sympathy toward the resistance.*

A few seconds later, Arus responded.

Arus: *Excellent. We will send a fabricator and jansha healing device now that you have secured lodging. We will send you items to set up localized surveillance of the King properties.*

He sent Arus a thank-you reply and then locked the communication device inside one of the air vents near the front door. Humans tended to look under mattresses and inside bathrooms for hidden items, but never in vents by the entrance. It felt too vulnerable, but that was what made it a perfect hiding spot. It would be only a matter of minutes before a small drone-like device flew here to his apartment to deliver his other requested technology.

He put the sheets and pillows on the bed and retrieved a couple of thick blankets from the closet. When he got into the bedroom he noticed the window was open and on his bed lay a parcel of small items. The drone had already come and gone in his absence of a mere thirty seconds. After he was done hiding the Krinar technology and laying the blankets on his bed, he went downstairs and knocked on Harper's door. Even though this was a bad idea, he couldn't deny the appeal of having the little Earth human all to himself in her living space. The subtle intimacy excited him. Maybe he could steal a kiss. One kiss from a human wouldn't put his mission in jeopardy, would it?

CHAPTER 3

Why the hell am I so nervous?

Harper didn't want to analyze the answer to that question too closely. She opened her apartment door, and Seth stepped inside. She moved back, as he dwarfed her in the doorway. He had to be close to six foot seven. Her head didn't even come close to the top of his shoulders. She had to admit she liked that, *a lot*.

Seth faced her and inhaled deeply. "Smells good." For a second she thought he was smelling *her*, and a shiver of delight rippled through her despite herself.

Harper forgot all about the food as she took in the sight of his muscular body. His shoulders strained at the edges of his red plaid button-up shirt, yet he was perfectly proportioned with a trim waist, the kind of waist a woman wanted to wrap her legs around. But that was a dangerous thought. He moved deeper into her apartment with a panther's grace, and she didn't doubt his rough-and-tumble side after having watched him deck that asshole earlier tonight.

"I...thanks." Harper tried to remember that he was commenting on her food, and she rushed past him back toward the kitchen. She had grilled some chicken breasts on a skillet with oil, lemon, and rosemary and put together a basic salad. She wasn't a pro, but she had mastered a few recipes to keep her from hitting the fast-food joints too often.

"Chicken?" Seth leaned his elbows on the tall bar that formed part of her kitchen as he watched her.

"Yeah. I know the Ks shut down the chicken and beef production plants, but I know a guy. He has free-range chickens, cattle, and goats. He sells eggs and meat products and goat cheese to the local families. That's not illegal, so the Ks haven't shown up to stop him."

Seth's eyes glittered, and he chuckled. "A town of rebels? I like it."

Harper almost told him he was more right than he realized. She considered telling him about the local resistance, even though she wasn't a part of it. It was pointless fighting the Ks, causing unrest and more violence. It wasn't the answer. The Ks weren't evil—it wasn't like they were bent on destroying the world. But they hadn't been forthcoming with their motivations either. Harper wanted to believe that if the humans and the Krinar could just meet and really talk a few things out, it could go a long way. But the Krinar were so secretive. It was hard to trust a race of aliens who wouldn't talk to you and treated you like misbehaving children.

She focused on Seth again as she cut the chicken into strips and placed them on top of the salads. He was classically handsome, with a strong jaw and aquiline nose, but his lips were a little too full, making him look sensual rather than statuesque. They looked kissable and tempting. She didn't want to focus on his eyes because if she did, she would daydream about their deep, rich blue color. Right now they were almost a rich China blue, but earlier she had seen a darker, stormier color in them at the bar when he had defended her.

"So, Seth. Where are you from?" She kept her tone casual because he was watching her a little too keenly, like a man who was contemplating the risks and rewards of making a move on her. That would be trouble. There was nothing better and in some ways nothing worse than being the sole focus of a gorgeous man.

"I'm from everywhere. Military brat. Dad was in the army. Can't seem to shake the travel bug out of my system." He shot her a half-cocked smile, somewhere between a grin and a sexy smirk, something that always tore a woman between wanting to kiss a man or slap him.

Damn, this Seth guy was dangerous. She tugged at the neck of her T-shirt, feeling the telltale flush of arousal flare inside her. Why hadn't she changed into something more attractive?

No. Bad Harper. You can't sleep with him, so there's no reason to dress up.

"Army, huh? How about your mom?"

"She's an accountant. My dad's retired, but she still runs a small office. They live in Boulder now." Seth picked up the two salad bowls and took them to the already set kitchen table, his body lightly brushing against hers from behind. A flare of excitement and wild heat passed between them, and her breath hitched. "Come and sit," he said. "I bet you've been on your feet all day." He swept his eyes down her body, pausing on her feet still in her strappy sandals before he met her eyes. Harper sucked in a breath. She could've sworn his scorching gaze almost touched her in a tangible caress.

"Thanks. I am pretty beat," she admitted. "You want a beer or wine?" She started for the fridge again.

Strong hands caught her by the waist and steered her back toward the table.

Normally she would have hated it if a man tried to steer her around like that, but when Seth took control, somehow it was like he was caring for her, spoiling her.

What a strange and...wonderful thought. Maybe he wasn't like Xander after all.

"Allow me," Seth said, his eyelashes sliding down to half-mast in that purely male, bedroom way that sent her into a wild flash of arousal. She was sucked in by the seductive lure of his rich baritone voice.

Okay... This man seemed to have been created out of thin air from the fantasies of women around the world. That meant something about him had to be wrong. He had to be a womanizer or married or something. After all, what did they say about when something looked too good to be true?

The last thing she needed was to be in another relationship, but if she could have one night of fun with him, why not? There was something about him that promised long, sweaty nights and sweet, intimate mornings. Things she'd once longed for in a relationship and now feared. Because good-looking men couldn't be trusted not to stray, and she couldn't trust herself not to be the fool who got her heart broken again and again.

She sat down at the table and had the good fortune of watching him bend over a little to reach for a bottle of wine inside her fridge. Damn, those jeans fit his body just right. It made her thirsty just to look at him. He quickly found a bottle of shiraz and two glasses. He handed her one and sat down opposite her at the table.

"So, what are your plans if you're just passing through?"

"I'm hoping to work for a bit and then head to Colorado, maybe settle down."

Harper took a bite of her salad and watched him spear a piece of chicken on his fork and look at it in momentary concern before he ate it.

"Do you like it? Is it too dry?" She immediately felt like an idiot. She shouldn't care if he didn't like her cooking. She wasn't lacking in self-confidence, at least not in general terms.

"It's surprisingly good. I'm not usually a fan of grilled chicken, but this is fantastic." Her shoulders lowered as she released the tension in them.

"Relax, Harper. I'm not going to bite," he teased her.

She choked on a swallow of her wine. "What?"

He took another bite, watching her as he chewed and swallowed. "You look half-terrified of something. I'm not some secret food critic. I'm just a man." He chuckled as if at some private joke.

"I'm not terrified of you," she argued.

"Really?" He quirked a brow, still grinning at her.

"Really. I'm just not used to having guys over lately. I don't even know why I invited you."

The smile didn't let up. "So you don't do this for all your brothers' new hires?"

"Not at all." That was the thing that was bothering

her. Even when she was dating, she preferred to spend the night at the man's place, not hers. Her apartment, even though it was small, was her refuge. Her Fortress of Solitude. It was decorated with her favorite pictures of the London and Paris skylines and other places she feared she would never be able to see. There just wasn't money to spend for a trip like that, and her savings always ended up going somewhere else. So her home was off-limits to the men she casually dated.

"You're just sweet, that's all," he replied. "Sweet and brave. I saw you stand up to that man tonight. You weren't scared of him at all, just pissed, but you barely showed it."

"I could have handled him if I hadn't been outnumbered. But I'm not an idiot." She hated how frosty her tone sounded right now, but she was used to defending her actions because her brothers always assumed she couldn't take care of herself.

"I never said you were." He finished off his wine as though it were a glass of water. He was not even buzzed. If she tried to keep up with him, she'd be swaying on her feet in a matter of minutes.

He finished his salad and put his plate in the sink after cleaning it. Something that simple should not have turned her on, but damn, it totally did. Then he took the bottle of wine and put it back in the fridge.

"I can clean up," she said quietly. "You should get

settled. If you have a car, you can park it outside the garage tomorrow."

"Thanks." He started to leave but paused as he noticed the artwork on her wall. He approached one black-and-white photo in particular. It was of the Notre-Dame cathedral in Paris from before the fire that had ravaged it in 2019. The fire had ruined the nine-hundred-year-old structure, devastating the world with its loss. The art and relics inside had been rescued, but some of the priceless stained-glass windows were gone forever.

He reached up to touch the towers, the only parts that hadn't collapsed in the raging inferno. "This was taken before the fire, wasn't it?"

"Yes. My parents went to Paris for their honey-moon. Mom loved the cathedral. She and my dad went to Mass there." Harper's voice thickened as she joined him in front of the framed print.

Pictures were the only way she felt she could relate to the world without headaches. Words were hard to read, which meant she relied heavily on audiobooks to read. But photos truly were worth a thousand words. When she looked at the Notre-Dame, she saw the past, she saw her parents, she saw beauty, faith, and devo-tion, not necessarily one of religion but to culture. And so much of it was gone, carried away on the winds over the Seine.

"If the Krinar had been there, they could have saved it."

"The Krinar would have tried to save it?" That surprised her.

"Yes, they could have put out much of the flames. The roof was made of nine-hundred-year-old timber, and much of the pews and altars in the church interior were all made of wood. But they could have stopped it if they'd been there. They value human culture." Seth's gaze was solemn and distant in a way that stirred Harper's heart. Whoever this man was, he had a connection to the cathedral on some level, the same way she did because of her parents.

"Were you ever there? Did you see it before the fire?" She didn't stop herself as she reached out and put a hand on his arm.

A world-weary sigh escaped his lips. "I saw it a year before the fire. I never quite got over the reality that what I saw so clearly and looked as if it would last forever is gone." He shook his head and turned toward her. "Thank you for dinner, Harper." He changed the subject so abruptly that she was caught off guard when he leaned down and kissed her.

With a gentle brush of those soft, warm lips over hers, an electric pulse sparked between them. Harper reached up to curl her arms around his neck without thinking. His kiss was a force of nature—raw, sensual, demanding, yet coaxing as he assaulted her senses. Hints of leather and sandalwood mixed with a clean scent that reminded her of fresh laundry and rain. He tasted like the shiraz they'd shared, sweetening her tongue in response.

He groaned and lifted her up by her waist, carrying her to the kitchen counter, where he set her down, bringing her closer to his height. She parted her legs, and he stepped in between them, like an ancient dance they had done a thousand times before. Heat pooled in her belly as a wave of sensual fire carried her away with building pleasure. He threaded a hand in her hair and cupped the back of her head as he devoured her lips.

God, it felt like heaven to be kissed like this, and Seth was a *master*. She was consumed by him, the way his hands roamed reverently down her back to her hips, the way he caressed her hair as though she were precious to him, but his kiss was open-mouthed and raw, dirty in the best possible way. A girl couldn't help but get turned on by this, so much so that it hurt. She whimpered against his lips, desperate in a way she hadn't been in a long time, with a need born of a longing and hunger she'd never felt before now. All of her previous lovers paled in comparison to this man and how he made her feel.

"Bedroom, *now*," she hissed and clawed at his back, wanting to drag him closer to her. He separated their bodies with a soft pop of their lips and cupped her face in his hands.

"You are tempting me in ways I've never been tempted before, but we can't. Not tonight." He licked his lips, and his eyelashes fanned as he blinked almost dazedly, staring intensely at her mouth. "But soon." He whispered the words with such sensual promise that she trembled with excitement.

"Soon," she echoed, still a little stunned that she had just tried to take him to bed when she barely knew him.

"I want to know you, *all* of you. Inside and out." He brushed the pad of his thumb over her lips, and she closed her eyes, savoring his touch. It felt so good she almost cried. Had it really been that long since she had let a man touch her like this? With such intimacy? Not just to get her in bed? Not in the last couple of years, it seemed. The realization made her eyes fill with tears, and before she could stop herself, she was crying.

Seth wrapped his arms around her, and she burrowed against him. Despite the pain inside her, her thoughts were dancing drunkenly around her head. She had held on to so much hurt, so much loss for so many years. Not even her brothers knew what she'd been burying all this time. Yet this man holding her had broken down her defenses with one searing kiss.

"Hush..." He pressed his cheek against the crown of her hair. Then she was carried into her bedroom as though she weighed nothing at all. He set her down and turned to study her dresser.

"Pajamas?" he asked in a soothing voice.

She sniffled, hating how vulnerable she was in that moment, but the tears still flowed freely down her face, and she couldn't make them stop. "Top drawer."

He came over and handed her the pajamas, then pulled back her comforter and sheets. She got up and headed for the bathroom to change, but then she paused at the doorway.

"Please don't go. It's not about sex. I just..." *I just want to be held.* She thought it with such agonizing sorrow that it made her body burn with shame. This level of vulnerability was too much for her.

"I'll stay," he promised and settled back on her bed.

She rushed into the bathroom, changed, brushed her teeth, and wiped a cleansing cloth over her face before she came back into the bedroom. She hoped the puffiness around her eyes would go away soon. There was nothing worse than being near a gorgeous man and looking like crap.

Seth lay on his back now, still fully clothed. He nodded at the empty side of the bed in silent invitation. She came over on anxious tiptoes and climbed into bed, turning off her nightlight. Silence settled in the room. Her heart pounded as she turned toward him, and even though he lay on top of the covers on the other side of her bed, he cocooned her, as if he knew that was exactly what she wanted.

"Good night," she whispered, the tears finally starting to dry upon her cheeks.

"Good night...Queenie."

Ordinarily she never would have let anyone call her that. That belonged to her mother. But when *he* said it, it felt like a promise, a vow, an endearment, and a hundred other intimate things that made her chest tighten and hope blossom inside her.

Whoever you are, Seth, you're already making me fall in love with you. And I swore I'd never do that again.

***

Sef lay awake long after Harper had fallen asleep, his mind racing and replaying that kiss over and over. Somehow, the human female had gotten even deeper under his skin than before. He was mere hours into this mission, and already he was losing control of himself. He knew he should contact Arus, perhaps have another guardian assigned to the Kings, but he didn't want another Krinar male anywhere near Harper. The mere thought of it choked him with possessive fury.

Was this how his brother had felt about the president's daughter Bianca? The woman he had betrayed his very position to woo? It was no wonder why they had come to blows over her. Sef had been ordered to remove her from Soren's presence before they became too attached, but it had been too late. Once a Krinar had claimed a charl, they became highly territorial and fiercely possessive.

He was already feeling that way now about Harper. Damn it all.

He held her until just before dawn, then carefully and silently slipped out of her bed and wrote her a note, leaving it in view on the pillow next to her before he left. Instead of returning to his room, however, he pulled out a small device from his jeans that could unlock any door and used it to pass through the garage and into King's Bar.

Sef took an hour placing small microdot cameras in key locations inside the bar and the storeroom. The storeroom was quite large, and ten chairs had been set up for a meeting. By the looks of things, the meeting had already been held. Sef took a mental note of the number for his next report. Ten rebels. Mason, Liam, and eight others, and they had connections to other rebel movements throughout the United States. He needed faces, though. The cameras would pick up their faces, and they could be run through the Krinar databases, which had access to all of the United States' identification systems—not that the Americans were aware of that fact. They could run driver's license photos, passports, thumbprints, criminal mug shots, all of it. Then they could track their past movements and see just how far this infestation had really spread.

He would figure out who the other rebels were and then determine how to proceed. Whatever he did, though, it would hurt Harper. At the very least, her brothers would be taken into Krinar custody for threat evaluation. If they were determined to be beyond rehabilitation, they would have their minds wiped and be reeducated to remove the danger they posed to his people. Such was the way of things.

Harper would lose her brothers, or at least lose the men she had known. They would become different people. It was a harsh punishment, but it was necessary to protect lives, both Krinar and human. The sooner the humans trusted the Krinar and accepted them and let them maintain control of certain things, the better off everyone would be.

Except for Harper. She would never forgive him. That shouldn't have chilled the blood in his veins and made him dread the future, but it did.

WANT TO KNOW WHAT HAPPENS NEXT WITH HARPER AND *Seth? Grab your copy HERE!*

ABOUT THE AUTHOR

USA TODAY Bestselling Author Lauren Smith is an Oklahoma attorney by day, who pens adventurous and edgy romance stories by the light of her smart phone flashlight app. She knew she was destined to be a romance writer when she attempted to re-write the entire *Titanic* movie just to save Jack from drowning. Connecting with readers by writing emotionally moving, realistic and sexy romances no matter what time period is her passion. She's won multiple awards in several romance subgenres including: New England Reader's Choice Awards, Greater Detroit BookSeller's Best Awards, and a Semi-Finalist award for the Mary Wollstonecraft Shelley Award.

To connect with Lauren, visit her at:
www.laurensmithbooks.com
lauren@Laurensmithbooks.com

OTHER TITLES BY LAUREN SMITH

Historical

The League of Rogues Series

Wicked Designs

His Wicked Seduction

Her Wicked Proposal

Wicked Rivals

Her Wicked Longing

His Wicked Embrace

The Earl of Pembroke

His Wicked Secret

The Last Wicked Rogue

Never Kiss a Scot

The Wicked Earls Club

The Earl of Pembroke

The Seduction Series

The Duelist's Seduction
The Rakehell's Seduction
The Rogue's Seduction
The Gentleman's Seduction

The Sins and Scandals Series
An Earl By Any Other Name
A Gentleman Never Surrenders
A Scottish Lord for Christmas

Standalone Stories
Tempted by A Rogue

Contemporary
Ever After Series
Legally Charming

The Surrender Series
The Gilded Cuff
The Gilded Cage
The Gilded Chain
The Darkest Hour

Love in London
Forbidden
Seduction
Climax
Forever Be Mine

Paranormal
Brothers of Ash and Fire
Grigori
Mikhail
Rurik
The Lost Barinov Dragon (coming soon)

Dark Seductions Series
The Shadows of Stormclyffe Hall

The Love Bites Series
The Bite of Winter
His Little Vixen (coming Fall 2019)

Brotherhood of the Blood Moon Series
Blood Moon on the Rise (coming soon)

Sci-Fi Romance
Cyborg Genesis Series
Across the Stars

The Krinar World
The Krinar Eclipse by Lauren Smith
The Krinar Code by Emma Castle